Finding Love for the Loner

Matchmaking Moms of Oceanview Church, Volume 2

Laurie Larsen

Published by Random Moon Books, 2020.

Copyright
Finding Love for the Loner
Copyright 2020 by Laurie Larsen
Published by Random Moon Books

All rights reserved. No part of this book may be used or reproduced in any manner whatsoever without written permission of the author except in the case of brief quotations embodied in critical articles or reviews.
All content by author Laurie Larsen
Cover Art by Steven Novak
E-book ISBN: 978-0-9975630-8-5
Paperback ISBN: 979-8-6371839-7-5
Published in the United States of America

Moms Go the Distance!

The Matchmaking Moms are in for a tough job finding a romantic match for Lily's son Winston. Gun-shy from love due to past rejections, he's built a life around his job, his dog and his online videogame prowess. He's perfectly happy, thank you very much. Except Lily knows his life will be better when the moms find a perfect match for him.

Rose is the matchmaker for the job, finding Tina, a fellow dog lover. Will the two of them connect, and if they do, will they be able to get past Winston's solitary ways, and Tina's need for control?

Chapter One: Winston's Normal

IT WAS STILL DARK OUT.

Winston Adams knew it was way earlier than he'd care to wake up on a Saturday. But his bedmate had stirred beside him and when she did that, it was only a matter of time until he was up, like it or not.

He closed his eyes again and lay still, hoping beyond hope that she'd settle back in.

She released an annoyed growl. No words, but he knew exactly what she meant.

He rolled over to face her, wrapped his arm around her and shushed her restlessness. "Shhh, baby, he whispered. "Go back to sleep. It's so nice and warm in here."

Something thumped against the mattress, most likely her tail, and a sloppy, wet tongue licked his face. "Okay, okay, calm down." At the sound of his voice, she pulled herself up to all fours, trapping him under her body. She bathed his face full force. "Rebel! Stop it! Okay! I'm up!"

Winston rolled off the bed and onto his feet, his ninety-pound yellow Labrador bounding behind him, landing on the wooden floor. The pads of her feet slid across the slick surface, and she slammed clumsily into the wall. She woofed, shook her great muscular form and headed for the bedroom door. Winston opened it and she escaped. The sounds of her bounding down the stairs filled the small two-story Cape Cod.

Glancing over his shoulder wistfully at the still-warm tousled bed, Winston sighed. It wasn't going to happen. Once his Rebel was up, she was up, and there was no rest for the weary, AKA him.

Two hours later, their morning routine was complete. He'd let Rebel out in the fenced-in yard to do her business while he'd dressed in sweats, a warm shirt and shoes. He put her in her harness, attached a leash and headed out for their two-mile walk. Back at the house, he measured out the large breakfast serving of dog food, and after gulping it down, she was ready for her lazy time. She'd leaped up on the couch, which was unfortunately shabby from her doing that day after day.

And the sun had come up. Finally.

Winston drew a hand over her short-haired back. "You know, most working people who have weekends off actually sleep in on Saturdays. Till, oh I don't know, eight o'clock at the earliest." Gone were his bachelor days of sleeping till noon. Once he'd become a puppy-daddy, his entire life revolved around the dog.

Rebel stretched out on the couch, occupying two thirds of it. Winston didn't mind relegating himself to the remaining third. It was time for his daily dose of online video games while she napped. He went to the TV, selected his game for the day, Star Battler, his favorite, an outer space-based battle game. In it, he was a fighter pilot, racking up points for destroying his enemies. Its graphics were phenomenal. He hooked up all his devices and returned to the couch. As he powered up, he peeked surreptitiously at the dog. Grinning, he nodded. Eyes closed, deep sigh. Soon she'd be snoring.

He donned his headphones and logged on with his handle, Win4Me, letting his partners around the world know that he was on. Soon, one by one, they joined him. His online group of friends never let him down. Familiar voices of people he'd never met from all over the globe soon filled his headphones. Although he'd never laid eyes on them, he'd spent hours of the most satisfying and exciting hours of his life with them. He entered into the game, readied his arsenal of weapons, and fired up his star fighter plane.

"Are we ready?"

"Ready, Captain."

"LookyCookie, you got the better of me last time. Not this time, buddy."

All sports involved trash talk and Winston grinned at the videogame version. He'd played sports in his childhood, so he was familiar with the practice. The online version was different, tamer, and not face-to-face, yet the concept was the same.

Winston sat in his recliner, watching his companions' tags pop on the screen. His comrades gathering here in this certain spot of the web at a designated time to join into a battle. A pretend battle, sure, but for him, and for all of them, he guessed, it surpassed a simple occasional game. When the countdown ended and the game started, they transported from their living rooms and their recliners. They became fighter pilots with the world's safety in jeopardy. They'd all demonstrated their willingness to sacrifice for their countries by engaging in the highest levels of training. They put their lives on the line every day and night to save the world from the bad guys.

Sounds of the fight filled his ears, his headphones cutting out noise beyond the battle. As Captain, he communicated orders to his star battlers. He heard their spoken messages in their individual planes. They were a team, in it together. One goal, one mission. Save the world from evil. The stakes could not be higher.

His big-screen TV displayed all the visuals he needed to direct the battle. It ceased to exist as simply the entertainment center of his house. It transformed into Battle Central, a vital tool to fight the evil ones.

The numbers on the screen, visible to everyone, counted down to their start time. "Brave fighters," Winston spoke. "You have answered the call to fight for justice and goodness in our world. With you beside me, and with all of us engaged, I know we can emerge victorious today. Are you ready?"

One by one, all his team members answered in the affirmative. The fight began.

Winston flew his plane into the vast open sky, escalating up and up beyond the altitude of airplanes, further up into the stratosphere where space battles engaged. "Win4U approaching enemy fighter one," he said confidently into his headphone.

"Roger, Win4U," responded several members of his team.

Winston accelerated, positioning his fighter plane on the tail end of the enemy. The opposing pilot was skilled, Winston knew this, not only from personal observation, but he knew this player's reputation and it was strong. That's why he'd taken him on as his own. Winston maneuvered to stay on his tail, up, down, flipping upside down and back upright again. Together, they avoided other battlers in the region, as well as meteors flying unexpectedly through the air. One collision with a huge chunk of rock would be the end for the pilot, but Winston had done this too many times. He knew how to make progress with his course without being detracted by random distractions.

Approval and encouragement from his teammates transmitted through his ears, and Winston edged a little further forward, carving down the distance between him and his target. Once, he was close enough to shoot but an opposing aircraft intervened, blocking his path. Only Winston's quick reflexes saved him from sure disaster.

Winston was in the zone, a place within the game that didn't rely on intentional actions. His senses had taken over. His intuition led the fight and he was along for the ride. Barriers threw themselves in front of him, and he dodged. He used his controls to maneuver his plane up, down, left, right, and the distractions were avoided. His single-minded goal was eliminating the enemy, no matter the risk to himself or his aircraft.

Battle scenes and sounds filled his senses, his pulse calm and his mind sharp. He had no idea how long he'd been tailing Enemy Number One when suddenly, he was right there. Win4U let loose a stream of artillery and struck the enemy in the back of his plane. A burst of flames shot forth, followed by endless smoke. The plane dropped from the sky.

A wave of excitement exploded through his headphones, applause and shouts of joy and congratulations from his teammates. His heart raced, now that the danger had passed and he had emerged from the zone.

This, right here. This is why he did this. This was the validation he sought.

"Thanks, team. Thank you. Now, let's go get the next one."

At two pm, Winston's stomach gurgled so loud he could no longer ignore it. He was hungry. He typed his farewell to his game buddies and signed off. Bleary-eyed, he stumbled to the kitchen. Rebel awoke and followed him. He looked down at her. "Yeah girl, I'm in the kitchen, and you know what that means."

He opened the cabinet and tossed her a dog treat. She caught it with one swoop of her powerful jaws. Then he began the search for something to feed himself. This dilemma was often a challenge. He wasn't much of a cook, but on the occasion he did prepare food, it was on a weekend. That way he could make a big batch and box up servings to take to work for lunch, or warm up for dinner after a long day. Considering it was Saturday, all his leftovers had been consumed.

He pulled open the freezer. It was empty, no surprise. Another challenge of being single was that you had to do all your own grocery shopping. Something Winston didn't relish. He dreaded pushing a cart through aisle after aisle, wondering what to buy.

So. He was down to two options: go out for fast food or make a peanut butter sandwich. He opened the cabinet. The bread still looked relatively fresh. Well, mold-free. He grabbed the peanut butter and made a few sandwiches.

As he sat and ate, he grabbed his phone. Two voicemails had arrived while he'd been gaming. He listened to them. Work asking if he'd consider working a few hours overtime tomorrow. He groaned. He could always use the money but he needed the leisure time more.

He'd think about it.

The other voicemail was from Mom. Although he always enjoyed chatting with his mom, his empty stomach was hoping she was calling to invite him over for dinner. He placed the call.

"Hey Mom."

"Sweetie! How are you? Enjoying your day off?"

"Yeah, although I got a call asking me to work tomorrow."

"All day?" Her voice sounded disappointed.

"No, just a few hours, and I could log in from home."

"Any time you want?"

He shrugged. "Yeah. They're pretty flexible. We just need to pound through some inventory."

"You could do it early in the morning and still make church at ten."

Winston rolled his eyes with amusement. His mother was always trying to get him to go to church. Not that he had anything against it. He definitely believed in God and prayed frequently. He just wanted two days a week where he didn't have to drag himself out of bed, prepare himself and head out the door. He loved his weekend free times. "We'll see, Mother. Hey, are you making dinner tonight?"

"Of course. Want to come over?"

"I thought you'd never ask." They set a time, chatted about a few other things, and ended the call. While he was at it, Winston called into his work contact, agreeing to work three hours overtime in the morning from home. Part of adulting was recognizing opportunities to make extra money, and what would he be doing anyway? More Starfighter?

He finished his meager lunch and harnessed Rebel back up for their afternoon walk. "Let's hit the road, baby girl." She wagged her tail and woofed.

• • • •

ONE THING ABOUT GOING to Mom's house for dinner was that she made him feel like a king. She waited on him hand and foot. Another thing was a guaranteed home cooked meal. Eating Mom's meals while growing up, he never really thought about it one way or the other. He'd never considered the effort it took for her to work all day, shop for food, decide what to make, prepare the meal, and have it on the table in time for dinner. Every. Single. Night. But now that he was an independent grown up, it'd begun to dawn on Winston how much his parents had done for him all his life. His dad coaching every sport he'd participated in. His mom attending every game. Throwing birthday parties for him. Making a big deal out of Christmas. He'd had a dream childhood.

Mom pulled a baking dish out of the oven and a heavenly aroma instantly filled the kitchen. "Mmm, that smells delicious," he said admiringly.

"Thanks. Just a chicken broccoli and cheese casserole." Mom tried to push it off as no big deal, but he knew she appreciated whatever compliments he offered.

"Hope you'll have leftovers for me to take home."

"Of course. I'll wrap up whatever we don't eat and it's yours."

"Hey now," Dad argued. "That'd make a great lunch tomorrow." He patted Winston on the shoulder. "Good to see you, son."

"Okay, okay. You don't have to fight over my food. James, I'll save a serving for us for lunch, and give the rest of Winston."

It was settled. Winston calculated in his mind. He'd get at least four meals out of the casserole, which meant he could wait till Tuesday to go grocery shopping.

Maybe he should look into those grocery delivery services. On the other hand, they were probably pricey.

They dug into dinner. Winston knew that dinner at the parents' could guarantee the discussion of at least three topics: the possibility of his attendance at church, his plans for home improvement projects, and any prospects of meeting a woman. They covered the first two while they ate the casserole. The third, his mom saved until she pulled out a steaming apple pie. As she cut it and scooped on vanilla ice cream, Winston's mouth watered.

"Are there any girls at work that you're interested in?" she asked casually, scooting the delectable plate in front of him.

Fortunately, his dad saved him from an immediate response. "Lily, give the guy a break, would ya? I'm sure if there are girls at work or anywhere else that he's interested in, he wouldn't necessarily tell his mother about it."

His mother was undeterred and turned back to him. "Winston, you have to realize that you are a real catch to the right woman."

Winston rolled his eyes while he shoveled baked goodness into his mouth.

His mother persisted. "Seriously. Listen to the facts. You have a college education. A steady job. You own your own home, car. You're fun, friendly, handsome. And you value family."

"Mmm, hmmm."

"What woman wouldn't want to date you?"

He pushed the empty plate away. "Mom, I don't know what to tell you. You see me as a catch. Girls my age don't. As much as you find it hard to believe, I don't have women lining up at my door dying to go out with me."

His mother sighed. "But there must be one. One, Winston. One nice young lady who is friendly and interested. Have you found *one* that you can invite out for coffee or dinner?"

"Nope. Not one." He'd love to think he could shut down the line of questioning by avoidance, but he knew she'd keep going.

"I find that very hard to believe, honey. You work in a big office with at least six hundred employees. Half of those have to be women."

"They're all married," he said, having no idea if it was true or not.

"Can't be. I have a challenge for you. Go into work on Monday and make it a goal to discover one single woman your age. Just one. Then, invite her to join you in the break room for ten minutes of conversation. See how it goes."

He clenched his mouth shut. It sounded easy, he had to admit. But just the thought of it caused his anxiety level to increase. He had no problems talking with women who considered him a friend. In social and work circles he was considered the fun guy, the one who made them laugh, the buddy. That, he was comfortable with. Everyone's best friend.

But escalating that to a romantic interest, nope. He'd experienced enough rejection to make him gun-shy. Granted, he hadn't opened himself up to a large quantity, but a small amount of rejection had more than taught him the lesson. He remembered painfully the time in high school he'd mustered up the courage to ask the girl he liked to a dance. They'd been standing at her locker. He'd had numerous fun conversations with her, right there. She'd always smiled when she saw him. He couldn't keep track of the number of times he'd made her laugh. But this time, her mouth dropped open, her eyes went wide and she was speechless. Until she finally said, "Oh, I'm sorry, Winston. I don't think of you like that. You're a great friend, but ..."

He'd brushed it off and chuckled and assured her, that was fine. They'd continue to be friends. No harm done. Oh, time for class, see ya, as he hustled off.

The memory of that rejection had kept him from asking anyone else out for the rest of high school. But college ... maybe that was a new opportunity. He'd attended a college with eleven thousand students. That meant that right outside his door were at least five thousand girls, none of whom knew about his humiliation in high school. Lots of guys he knew had success asking girls out. Why not him? He'd be that guy, in college. It was a new start.

As the first month of his freshman year proceeded, he made friends with several girls on his dormitory floor. He got to know them, established a conversational friendship. But he'd learned his lesson. He couldn't sink so firmly into friendship territory that they wouldn't think of him as boyfriend material. So four weeks in, he selected one of the girls, visited her room when he knew her roommate was out, mustered up his courage, and asked her out for a date.

Oh, she'd said, she was so sorry, she'd said. She wished he'd asked her just last week. But meanwhile, she'd started dating one of the other guys on the floor and she was hoping they'd become a steady couple.

No problem, he'd assured her. None at all. He'd made up a sudden appointment he needed to get to and dove out the door.

Why did this always happen to him? Was he always doomed to be "just friends" material? But over the next week, he steadied himself. Tried to talk some sense into his brain. This time was different. She hadn't said she wasn't interested in him as a boyfriend. It was more of a timing problem. If he'd asked her earlier, she may have said yes.

So maybe it was a numbers game? If he asked someone else, maybe the timing would be right. He needed to gather up his courage to ask someone one more time.

Over the next two weeks he paid particular attention to the dating habits of his female friends. Although there wasn't one he felt strongly about, he knew he had to give it a try, or he'd be stuck single the rest of his life. All skills took practice to develop. He'd practice now, with another girl.

Pain had probably dimmed the memory of her name, or even her face, but he'd found the moment to approach the girl four doors down, one he'd befriended in the first week of school. He'd decided to put some planning into the date. Maybe a fun invitation would entice a "yes" out of her. He picked up a red rose from the local florist, geared up his nerve, and knocked on her door. When she answered, he got right to it. Smiled, offered her the rose, asked her to join him for a nice dinner at a nearby steak dinner.

Her silence was a stab to his heart. His confidence shattered the longer it stretched out. Then, she cleared her throat, stuck her head out in the hallway, looked both ways, took him by the arm, pulled him into her room and shut the door. "Look, um," she stammered. "I appreciate you going to this trouble. I really do. But Winston, I just got over a bad break up, and I don't want to date right now. You can understand that, right? It's not you, honestly. I just want to be single. We can go as friends. We can still be friends, right?"

He agreed to everything, yes, yes, broken heart, want to be friends, stumbled out and never spoke to the nameless girl again. But three weeks later, he saw her at a dorm party and she had what looked like a boyfriend glued to her side.

That was it. The end. He'd prayed for acceptance of his fate as a single man. As much as he'd love to have a girlfriend, and he couldn't imagine his eventual future without a family, it must not be in God's plan for him. He'd learn to accept being single. Life would be so much easier without worrying about women anyway. After removing the stress of asking women out on dates, he enjoyed his college experience. He made friends, both male and female, and participated in lots of group social activities. When he'd gotten his job, despite his mother's advice, he couldn't care less which of his new co-workers was single or married. It didn't apply to him. He was friendly to everyone.

"Leave the poor guy alone, Lily," his dad said now, pulling him out of his morose thoughts. "He's got a lot of things on his plate with the job, Rebel, the house. He'll meet a woman when the time is right."

Winston winked at his dad and glanced at his mom. Amazingly, she looked willing to let the subject drop. Which wasn't like her. Maybe she'd finally given up hope like he had. No sense wishing for the impossible. "Just promise me one thing," she said. "If you get asked out by someone, just say yes. Just for the fun of it."

He chuckled with disbelief. "Oh, you mean the next time a beautiful woman pops up out of nowhere and asks me out on a date, I should say yes?"

She smiled happily and nodded.

He stood and took his plate to the sink, leaned in and kissed his mom's cheek. "It's a deal. Thanks for a fantastic meal, as usual. Whatcha got on TV tonight?"

He walked into the family room, where he'd watched a million shows during his lifetime, settled on to the couch and the comfort of his family.

Chapter Two: The Moms Regroup

LILY ADAMS SAT IN BIBLE Study at Oceanview Church. She tried to focus on the Apostle Paul's walk to Emmaus but her mind was on something else. Her next meeting, in fact. Her meeting with the Matchmaking Moms of Oceanview Church.

A few weeks ago she'd happened to be placed at a table at this very Bible Study with two other women. Reverend Harris instructed them to get to know each other and find one thing they all had in common. Something deeper than, we're all women. We're all mothers. We're all Christians.

So they went deeper. And they eventually discovered that they all had adult children who were striking out in the love department. They all had a son or daughter who needed a little nudge to find the right mate.

And the Matchmaking Moms of Oceanview Church had emerged.

Was it just coincidence that they were placed together? Random placement? No. Lily was convinced it was divinely inspired. They'd all individually prayed to God for those offspring to find help with love. Now, God was delivering.

The moms would orchestrate the effort. They would find a mate for each of these adult children stuck on pause. But it would be a secret endeavor so the subject and his or her match

FINDING LOVE FOR THE LONER 17

wouldn't know what was going on behind the scenes. And, each mom would help another, not matchmaking for their own child.

After weekly Bible Study, they would meet and discuss their mission. Provide support, information, ideas, encouragement. Keep the wheels turning. Today would start the journey for Winston and the future love of his life.

She managed to direct her attention back on Reverend Harris and jotted a few notes. When the lesson was over, she, Rose and Dahlia got down to business.

"So, ladies," said Lily. "How are we doing today? I'm excited to have our meeting. I saw Winston last night and I believe I primed the pump. Although he's not actively seeking out his own girlfriend, I got him to agree to being open if a new woman asked him out."

Rose Harmon clapped her hands. "Oh good. Let's get to work figuring out who that woman will be." In a planning meeting last week, Rose was assigned to be Winston's matchmaker.

Dahlia Benjamin, the third member of the Matchmaking team, sat down. "I'll listen to see if I can get any ideas, but what do you say we just focus on Winston at this meeting? It might get confusing if we kick off all three efforts at once."

The others agreed. Rose pulled out a fresh sheet of paper and uncapped her pen. "Okay, Mom," she said as she smiled at Lily. "Tell me about Winston."

Lily's heart overflowed talking about her one and only child, her handsome boy, her pride and joy. "He's always been such a good kid. He always made us proud. School wasn't always easy for him, and sometimes he was a little careless with his assignments. But he succeeded. He graduated from college, got a good job with a decent company and he works hard. They really like him there. They've promoted him several times and given him special assignments to work on."

Rose looked up from writing. "So at work he sounds like a superstar. Would you say he is at his most impressive at work?"

Lily thought about that. "Yeah, that's probably accurate. He must feel his most productive at work, and his confidence level must be pretty high."

Rose nodded. "Where does he work and what does he do?"

Lily gave her the company name and address. She did her best to describe his job tasks, although she wasn't entirely sure of his responsibilities. "He works for a manufacturing company that creates automotive parts. He works in the office and he manages certain work processes. He examines the processes both on the assembly line, in the office, the delivery of the parts, all of it, and tries to identify places to expedite."

Rose had been jotting down notes but had given up, instead staring at Lily with wide eyes.

"I know. It's not a glamour job. But it's a solid career, it pays pretty well and he does well at it."

Rose asked, "Do young women work there?"

Lily chuckled. "I don't honestly know, but I have to guess so."

Rose made an emphatic underline several times on her notes. "I'll check into it. But let's think of other strategies besides work. Just in case. Now, what are Winston's hobbies? What does he like to do?"

Lily was more enthusiastic now. This stuff, she knew. "He's a dog owner. He has a big yellow lab, Rebel. He does a lot with her because she needs a ton of exercise. He walks her, takes her to the dog park, hiking, swimming in the pond."

"Oh!" Rose exclaimed, putting pen to paper. "That's good! If I find a young woman who loves dogs, we could set up a date at the dog park. How easy would that be?"

"Sure!" Lily beamed.

"What else?"

"He likes to golf."

Rose frowned. "It's January which isn't really golf weather, even in the golf capitol of the world. Anything else?"

Lily sighed. "He spends hours of time every day on his online video games. He evidently has this big posse of players who meet up at certain times to play against each other."

"Online?"

"Yes, he doesn't know these people personally. They could be anywhere in the world. And he only knows them by their screen names."

Rose studied her face as she thought. "Hmmm. That isn't ringing any bells for ideas. What woman would be interested in video games, and how would I ever get the two of them together for a date?"

"I know. Welcome to my nightmare."

Rose tapped her pen on the pad. She turned to Dahlia. "Any thoughts from you?"

"I think your best bet is the dog angle."

"Agreed." Rose put an encouraging smile on her face and aimed it at Lily. "Let me get to work on this. I'll report back." She laid a hand on Lily's. "Don't worry, sugar. I'm gonna find the perfect dog-lovin' honey for your boy."

Chapter Three: Winston Goes to Work

Matchmaking Moms of Oceanview Church

WINSTON ARRIVED AT his cubicle, set his mega-mug of coffee on his desk, and stowed his lunch bag containing his mom's casserole in his drawer. He flipped on the computer.

"Good morning," said a voice behind him. He recognized his work buddy, Vanessa.

"Hey," he said.

"How was your weekend?" she asked. She came into his cubicle and rested her hip on the corner of his desk.

"It was good. How about yours?"

She shrugged. "Fine. But back to you. Did you do anything fun?"

"The usual."

Vanessa placed an index finger on her chin. "Translation: played with Rebel, played online games, maybe went to the parents' for dinner?"

Winston blinked. Was he that much of an open book? That easy to predict? "All right, smarty pants. Maybe I should do something crazy and completely out of character just to have something to report to you on Monday mornings."

"Yes! Now you're talking!" She lowered herself into the chair beside his desk. "What would you do?"

"Huh?"

"What would you consider out of character and crazy?"

Winston shrugged.

"No, tell me. I want to hear it."

"I don't know, Vanessa. Maybe jump out of an airplane? Climb to the top of a mountain? Scuba dive to the bottom of the ocean?"

Vanessa smirked, frowning at him. "You're hopeless, you know that?"

Winston looked at her, confused. "What do you mean?"

"None of your crazy ideas involve a woman, do you realize that? No wonder you're perpetually single. I'm beginning to think you're a confirmed bachelor. I'd say something crazy and out of character for you is to simply ask a woman out on a date."

"Oh yeah, that'd be crazy, wouldn't it?" He turned to his computer and noticed it was all warmed up and ready to go. "And what's wrong with being a bachelor? I can think of worse things in life."

Vanessa shook her head. "You've got too much to offer the right woman. I think you just need my help in hooking her."

Winston pointed at the screen. "Time to get to work, social butterfly. But thanks for thinking of me. And if I'm ever ready for you to set me up with someone, I'll let you know, all right?"

Vanessa smiled what looked to Winston like a devious smile. "Okay, bud. See you at lunch."

He waved her away and opened up his work queue. He spent a moment considering which task to tackle first, then glanced up when he realized Vanessa was lingering just outside his cubicle. "Ness?" he asked, then she smiled and walked away.

He watched her walk away, wondering. Then he went back to work.

Thirty minutes later, he was absorbed in his work. The sound of laughter rang in the background, but he ignored it. When he stopped midmorning to stretch his legs, he happened to run into one of his teammates, Clark.

"What's up, man?" Winston said as he left his cubicle.

"She got you good, didn't she?" Clark said with a grin.

"Who? What?"

"You haven't seen it? Take a look." Clark pointed at the exterior wall of Winston's cube, facing the main aisle. Winston came around and saw that someone had pinned a sheet of paper containing a handwritten note:

"*Looking for a woman. I'm a real catch. Attributes: I have a car and all my teeth. If interested, call Winston.*" It also included his cell phone number. He snatched it down and crumbled it in his hand. He shook his head at Clark. "Vanessa."

Clark nodded. "Yep."

Winston tossed the note in the trash and continued on. He assumed a brisk pace and walked through the aisles, the same route he took during every morning break. It was good to get his heart beating after several hours of sedentary work. Only this time, people who usually only vaguely noticed him while he passed their desks, occasionally offering a wave, snickered as he walked by. Some offered a comment, "Good one, Winston."

"Hope you find her."

Winston rolled his eyes. Vanessa must've placed the note in more locations than just his cubicle for so many people to be aware of it. He took a detour and directed his steps to Vanessa's cube.

"Very funny," he said when he arrived.

She burst out with a joyous laugh. "Have you got any offers?"

"No, although I have gotten lots of laughs at my expense. Where else did you put it besides pinned to my cube?"

She smiled and turned to her computer. She pulled up her Facebook page, where she'd posted a picture. Winston was sure she'd written some sarcastic caption but he didn't care to read it. "Take that down."

She laughed.

"Now, Vanessa, I mean it."

He turned and heard her say sadly, "Okay."

He made his way back to his desk. He sat and took a breath before diving back into work. It wasn't that he minded being the brunt of jokes, especially if they were well intentioned. He'd grown accustomed to being the comic relief for his friends. He was a good sport. And now that he was in his late twenties, and most of his friends had either gotten married, or at the very least, met the woman they would eventually marry, and he remained single with the perpetually empty dance card, so to speak, he unwittingly gave his friends plenty of material to tease him about.

He'd always laugh along. Wouldn't let it bother him. They'd eventually move on. But that didn't mean he had to like it. Vanessa had her little joke and had gotten some mileage out of it. It was done.

Chapter Four: Rose Hatches Her Plan

THIS WAS GOING TO BE easy-peasy. Winston loved dogs. She'd find a single young woman who loved dogs and she'd plan a chance meeting for the two of them. They'd bond over their canine companions and he'd ask her out for a cup of hot chocolate to warm up, and things would go from there.

Now, who would play the female role? Rose let her mind run free for a moment. Who are people that love dogs? Veterinarians, of course. Or, anyone who worked at a veterinarian's office. Weren't there assistants who worked in the vet's office? Professionals who greeted the patients, took their vitals, trimmed their nails, weighed them, got them ready for the doctor? She scanned her brain, trying to remember if any eligible young women worked at the vet's office they took their own Scamper to.

Suddenly she had an idea. You could find out just about anything on the internet. She went to the computer that sat on the desk in their sitting room and flipped it on. When it warmed up, she accessed the website to their veterinarian's office. Yes, there was a tab called Who We Are. The page brought up a list of pictures of everyone who worked in the office, along with short bios. She bypassed the two veterinarians ... one was a man in his forties, and the other was a woman currently off on maternity leave. But underneath those, there were at least ten other employees who performed other functions to keep the vet's office running smoothly.

She paged to the first attractive young female and read her bio. The writeup mentioned a husband, so she kept going. Towards the bottom Rose tapped the picture on the screen and said, "Bingo." The picture showed a fresh-faced woman with a happy smile. She wore her brunette hair long, and she was young and attractive. The bio read, "Tina Mitchell has loved animals since she was a child. She currently is the proud mama of a German shepherd, a maltese, a tabby cat and a parakeet. Her home is a little loud and crazy at times, but she loves being the only human in a kingdom of animals."

Rose pumped a triumphant fist into the air. "Pretty, young, single and loves animals. Perfect match for our Winston." She thought about calling Lily immediately, then decided against it. Tina was a great prospect, but Rose needed to put the first meeting plan into action.

She looked back at the website, absentmindedly tapping her fingernails in rhythm on the table. Tina was described as a vet tech, and when she found the list of duties that vet techs performed, she had an idea. Tina did nail clipping for dogs without an appointment. She could take her own little moppy-haired mutt, Scamper, ask for a nail clipping, and just tell the front desk attendant that she preferred Tina to do it because she'd done such a good job with Scamper in the past.

Thirty minutes later, she was standing at the front desk of the vet's office. "Tina, you say? Let me check her schedule." The woman there tapped on her computer. "Looks like she's finishing up a lab test. She should be free in a few minutes. I'll let her know you're here."

Rose smiled her best southern girl smile. "Thank you so much, you're so kind." She led Scamper over to the bench and sat. While she waited, she repeated a silent prayer, "God, please help me get these two young people together." She mentally ran through her To Do items for today's meeting. Besides getting Scamper's toenails clipped, she wanted to engage Tina in conversation, make sure she saw no red flags with setting her up with Winston, and make sure she hadn't gotten married since writing her website bio. Her heart raced with the enormity of this meeting's importance, but she closed her eyes and asked for God's strength. She'd get it done.

She had to.

"Scamper? Scamper Harmon?"

Rose chuckled and stood. "That's us." She walked forward, leading Scamper. She recognized Tina from her website photo. Although she'd told the little white lie to the front desk attendant that she'd worked with Tina before, they actually had never met. "Hi Tina," she said warmly nevertheless. She must meet so many dogs and humans every day, she could understand not remembering.

"Hello. Scamper and Mrs. Harmon? You're here for a nail clipping?"

"Yes. Scamper is quite particular but you've done such a good job before, I hope you don't mind I asked for you by name."

"Of course I don't mind." The young woman leaned down to Scamper's level. "Hi, Scamper." She gave the dog's curly white face a friendly pat. "Are those long nails giving you some trouble?" Tina picked up one of Scamper's paws and examined them. "Yes, it's time. Lead him on back here to Room 2."

They entered the room and Tina shut the door. "I find the little ones do the best if their family member holds them while I clip. Makes them feel secure."

"Great idea." Rose lifted Scamper, holding him in her arms, while her mind went through a checklist: kind, thoughtful. Tina reached for one paw and Scamper, fortunately, didn't fight the procedure, giving Rose opportunity to direct the conversation. "You must love animals to work in a vet's office."

Tina smiled, her cute cheeks bunching as she glanced up for a moment at Rose before looking back at her task at hand. "Yes ma'am, I sure do. I've loved animals my whole life. It's always been my dream to work with animals. In fact, I've worked here several years, gaining good experience. I'm actually thinking of applying to vet school myself."

"How wonderful, dear!" Rose enthused, thinking to herself: ambitious, smart. Then she pushed the envelope with the comment, "Does your husband support your decision to go back to school?"

Tina glanced at her and shook her head before gripping the next paw. "I'm not married. I'm hoping I can continue working here while going to vet school at night. We'll see. It's extremely competitive."

Rose could barely continue her smile: single. "Well dear, I'm sure you will get in with all your ambition and experience. You'd make a wonderful vet."

Tina gripped Scamper's final paw. "I pray every day for it all to work out. I'm just going down the path of faith. Okay, Scamper. You're all done! You should feel better now, boy."

Rose was over the moon: Christian. "I assume you have a dog of your own, Tina?"

Tina was tapping into a little handheld device. "Yes, ma'am, I have two. A big one and a little one."

Rose ventured out on faith herself. "I wonder if you would be interested in an event I'm putting together through the local Lions club I volunteer at. We're setting up a doggie social day at a local dog park. Just a two-hour event where dogs and owners can get together, socialize, get to know each other. We'll have a table with bottled water, cookies for the humans and treats for the dogs. Nametags so everyone can get to know each other. Would you be interested?"

Tina smiled and her pretty face was even prettier. "I sure would, as long as I'm not working. I'd probably take Roscoe, my German shepherd. He's always looking for exercise and he loves other dogs."

"Wonderful! I'll send you an invitation to you here at the vet's office. What are your normal days off?"

Tina shrugged. "It varies, but I normally have Tuesday nights off, and Sundays, since the office is closed." Tina led her out to the cash register. "They'll take your payment here, Mrs. Harmon. Good to see you."

Back in the car, Rose couldn't be happier with her progress. Tina was a dream and she knew Winston would love her. She was perfect.

The idea of the doggie get together just sort of came to her instantaneously, making her wonder if it was inspired by God. Maybe not, since it required telling a lie. But regardless, it was a way to get Winston and Tina together with their dogs. But she couldn't risk inviting a whole bunch of people. Winston and

Tina might never gravitate toward each other if left to chance. No, it had to be just Winston and Tina. Alone.

Chapter Five: Winston Receives an Invitation

Matchmaking Moms of Oceanview Church

ROSE WENT INTO A FLURRY of activity that afternoon. First she called the Dog Park and confirmed that it was open on Tuesday night at six pm. Then she pulled up the word processing program on her computer and tinkered with various color schemes, designs and doggie pictures. End result: a rather convincing-looking flyer for the Doggie/Human get together. She printed out two copies. Looking at it closely, she called Lily.

"I just wanted to let you know that Operation Winston – Tina is underway."

Lily sounded instantly excited. "Tina? Who's Tina?"

Rose explained her plan and everything she had done to get to this moment.

"Oh that's wonderful. The dogs would give them instant chemistry with a common interest. But how are you going to pull off a big event sponsored by the Lions? And what if Winston and Tina don't actually meet?"

"I don't want to leave it to chance, and you're right, I don't want to go through with planning a big public event. So I'll send out one flyer to Winston and one to Tina. They'll go there and see that no one else is there. Hopefully they'll bond over the absence of any other guests, leading to a pleasant evening, or at the very least, a conversation. The next day, the postman will deliver cancellation notices for the event, which are, oops, one day late."

Lily laughed. "I like it. By the way, you're devious. I like that too."

"Hey, it takes a little deceit to get these young folks set up, doesn't it?"

"I'll remember that when it's my turn to work on Dahlia's son, Micah."

Rose grinned. "Hopefully we'll have a success record by then." They chatted about their Bible study lesson for a few minutes, and then Rose said, "Well, I better get these to the post office. Don't say anything to Winston about the event unless he mentions it to you. Then, encourage him to go."

"You bet." Lily gave her Winston's address and hung up.

• • • •

WINSTON DROVE HOME from work, exhausted from a day of hustle, problem-solving and keeping his cool in the face of stress. Sitting at a red light, he calculated in his head: he was twenty-eight, he'd been working professionally for five years. Thirty-two years till he could retire with a company pension and Social Security.

That meant he had to keep working.

He groaned and pushed his accelerator through the green light. Whoever came up with the plan of having to work forty or fifty hours a week when you were his age? Why couldn't life work the other way around? Enjoy retirement for ten or fifteen years while you were young, then start your career when you were too old to have fun?

He arrived home, pulled into his driveway and then into his garage. He shook his head. In general, he didn't mind his job. It paid the bills and gave him the independence he'd always wanted. But long gone were the days of childhood when you had three months off from school in the summer, two weeks in the spring and a month over Christmas. If he could have that much time off now, he'd been much more content.

But only if he still got paid for not working. Maybe he should've been a teacher.

He pulled himself out of the car and prepared for the inevitable enthusiastic greeting he'd get from Rebel.

A loud thud against the door alerted him to the fact that Rebel had heard the garage door open and knew he would soon be appearing in the doorway. "Rebel, girl," he called.

Then the barking began. *Woof woof woof woof.* Winston smiled. He knew he should probably train that out of her, but heck, he enjoyed her excitement. Who else on earth would go this crazy just because he was coming home?

He swung open the door and she leaped into the air, into his open arms. She thrashed in her excitement and he laughed. "Okay, okay, girl. Yes, I'm home. I'm excited to see you too."

She reduced her barking to whimpering and her tongue flailed, occasionally meeting its mark on his face.

He lowered her to the floor and she led the way to the back door, looking over her shoulder to make sure he was following her. He waited while she sniffed in the corners of his fenced-in yard, did her business, and returned. Back inside, he sat on the couch and she bounded up beside him, walking over his lap, turning around, back again, and finally plopped down beside him. Her evening routine was complete, for the moment.

He reached for his remotes: one for the TV, one for the game system. He checked the time. Twenty minutes until his coordinated game started with his posse of online buddies. Powering everything up, he logged on and trotted to the kitchen. Rebel pounded after him. He poured a huge bowl of kibble for her and searched in the fridge for himself. He'd finished Mom's leftovers days ago and hadn't cooked anything himself since. He closed the fridge and opened the freezer. Bingo. Pizza it is.

He started the oven on preheat, opened the box containing a frozen pepperoni and walked back to the living room while Rebel made appreciative gulping sounds. She'd consume the two and a half cups of food in two minutes or less.

He looked at the lineup of players who'd logged in already and noticed a lot of the likely suspects. Five or six familiar names who joined him game after game. He slipped on his headphones and offered a few casual greetings to his rivals and smiled at their retorts. Typical game day threats. Nothing he'd worry about. In Star Battler, he'd worked up a better rating than any of his normal opponents. Every time he'd won, he'd registered the win with the game sponsors and as a result he was one of the highest-ranked Star Battlers playing the game. Not an achievement he shared with many people outside the online gaming world, because, after all, it was just a bunch of nerds playing video games together. Who else would care? But to these guys, he was a big deal. He was Win4U and they felt proud to be playing against him. He always gave them a good run and he didn't win every time. It made their day to actually beat him, but it didn't last for long. He always came back and won the next time. Practice made perfect, and he'd found something here in the online gaming world that he was really, really good at.

Too bad it was a solitary sport played while sitting on his couch.

Hearing a timer ding, he jogged into the kitchen and slid the pizza into the oven. He set the timer. He'd have time to pull it out and slice it before the game started.

He headed back to check on the game contestants and was surprised to see a new one log in.

"LeiaPower," he said out loud, reading the handle. Of course, the name made him think immediately of Princess Leia from Star Wars fame. He loved Star Wars and was a huge fan. He'd not only seen all the movies multiple times, and read the books they originated from, but he'd joined the fan sites that shared all the background information. He doubted if there was one accurate fact about the Star Wars universe that he didn't know.

He reached for his controller and rubbed it with his thumb, wondering if he should welcome this new player to his game. *His* game, because he was the highest ranked player. If this person had chosen Leia in her handle, two things must be true. 1 – she must be a female herself and 2 – she must be a Star Wars fan. And if those two things were true, Winston wanted to get to know this unusual female.

He slid on his headphones and said, "LeiaPower, welcome. Is your name reminiscent of Princess Leia?"

"Of course, is there any other?"

The voice was definitely female. The very sound of a woman's timbre filling his gaming headphones made him shiver. Winston laughed out loud. Feisty, she was. "Welcome to the game," he said.

"Had to check out the great Win4U."

He smiled, then his oven timer beeped, and he raced out to the kitchen, pulling his pizza out before the aroma of burnt cheese filled his house. He placed it on a wooden cutting board and while he gave it a few minutes to cool, he allowed his mind to wander to this LeiaPower player. He wondered what she looked like, where she lived, what she was like in person. Then, slicing the pizza into six pieces, he put them on a platter and carried them into the gaming room.

Rebel popped her head up from her paws when he walked in with the pizza. He sat beside her. "No girl, no stealing my dinner. This stuff's bad for you anyway." She gave him a mournful look with her big brown eyes and his heart melted a little. He tugged at a little mound of melted mozzarella, blew on it until it was cool and offered it to her. She devoured it in one fell swoop. "That's it, now. Big game tonight. We've actually got a woman joining us for Star Battler tonight. Let me concentrate."

He set the countdown timer, alerting all his competitors that the game was starting in 10, 9, 8, ... The customary adrenaline built in his chest and he rubbed his hands together. He glanced quickly at LeiaPower's avatar, a cartoon representation of a youngish Princess Leia from the movies and smiled. Gaming with a woman was unusual for him but it shouldn't change his game at all. He'd treat her like any other competitor and hopefully, he'd come out on top. He braced himself on the couch, gripped his controller and watched the countdown, 3, 2, 1 ... GO!

• • • •

FOUR HOURS PASSED LIKE a blink of an eye. The game had completed, for tonight anyway. It was an intense one. He'd won, finally, but his competitors had given him a run for his money. Were their skill levels that close, or had he been distracted by the new player, leaving his concentration subpar? He wasn't sure, but winning this particular battle wasn't as effortless as most of his others.

When they'd finished, LeiaPower shot him a wink-heart emoji onscreen and in his headphones, he heard, "Win4U did not disappoint." He managed to send her a thumbs-up emoji before she signed off. His heart pumped a little extra and he felt good as he turned off the game with a smile. "Let's go Rebel. Walk time."

The dog bounded off the couch, ran to the door, barking excitedly. He snapped her leash onto her collar and opened the door. They followed the two-mile trek he took her on every morning and every evening. She was a creature of habit and enjoyed the regularity, and it was good exercise since they'd both been sitting (or in her case, lying down) on the couch all evening. He gripped the leash a little tighter when they approached the fenced-in yard of a ferocious-sounding husky who always riled Rebel up a little bit. Fortunately, the husky wasn't out tonight. A mile or so in, Rebel got a little excited at a big tree they passed. One time, about three months ago, she'd chased a squirrel up that very tree, and every time they'd passed it since, she remembered that excitement, even though it'd never happened again.

Their walk done, he stopped at the mailbox and pulled out a handful of envelopes, then climbed up his front steps and into the house. He snapped off Rebel's leash and she headed straight for the water bowl. He dropped the stack of mail on the table. He and Rebel watched a short sit-com on TV, then headed up to bed, ready to start it all over tomorrow.

• • • •

"HAS WINSTON MENTIONED anything about the invitation I sent him?"

Lily frowned at the phone. "No, Rose. He hasn't, in fact."

She could hear Rose flipping through some papers. She read out an address. "Is that right?"

"Yeah, that's Winston's address all right. When did you send it out?"

It had been six days ago, by local mail. He definitely should've received it by now. "I'm sure he's gotten it. Why would he mention it to his mother?"

Rose sighed. "How do we make sure he's going? We don't want poor Tina to show up and no one else is there."

Lily tapped her lip with her finger. "I've got just the thing." She told Rose her plan and hung up.

Fifty minutes later, she had a piping hot pan of spaghetti pie on her car seat and was heading over to Winston's house. She knew what time he usually arrived home from work, and she scheduled her visit to beat him there by five minutes. Sure enough, sitting in her car outside his house, he pulled into his driveway, beeping his horn.

She got out, carrying the food.

"Hey Mom, nice surprise," he said with a happy grin and an embrace. He looked particularly handsome today, his brown hair and beard neatly trimmed, and the clothes he'd picked this morning for work were among the new ones he'd acquired at Christmas, fitting his slim form well. It warmed her heart knowing she could still put that smile on her son's face, even at his age. Being an only child, she'd spoiled and coddled him, probably even more than any other southern mama had her offspring. She couldn't help it. She'd fallen in love with the boy the second he was born. No, that wasn't true. She'd fallen in love the moment she knew she was carrying him. When she finally got to see his beautiful face, she was a goner.

They'd always gotten along, the two of them. Their personalities were similar in so many ways, although he got his competitiveness from his daddy. A good blend of them both, just like his looks. He had his dad's chestnut hair and her blue eyes. What a stunner he was.

"To what do I owe the pleasure, Mama?" he asked with his arm around her shoulder.

"Did you notice the pan in my hands?"

"Well, now that you mention it, it was either the pan or that heavenly aroma I smell."

She laughed. "Sorry for dropping in on you, but I was planning this spaghetti pie for Dad and I, and then he dropped the news that he had a dinner meeting, so I decided to drop in on my favorite son."

"Awesome. Come on in. I'll take Rebel for a quick walk and we can eat when I get back."

Lily nodded. "I'll set your table while you're walking." This was working out just fine. Knowing her son as she did, she was quite certain she'd have to shovel through a bunch of junk in order to set the table. Maybe somewhere hiding among the empty grocery bags, stacks of mail, and dog paraphernalia, she'd find Rose's phony flyer.

Rebel greeted her by placing her huge paws on Lily's shoulders and lapping her face with her wet, warm tongue. Lily closed her eyes and laughed, knowing Rebel's over-the-top attention was part of the experience. Rebel was her granddaughter, after all.

"All right, girl," Winston said, and they shuffled out the door.

Lily wiped off the slobber and went to the table. It was covered, as she expected, with *stuff*. Why oh why, she thought, as she often did when she visited, did her son tolerate this kind of disorder? She hadn't raised him this way! He must've learned it in college.

Pushing her negative thoughts aside, she focused on her task, determined to locate Rose's flyer before he returned. Then somehow direct his attention to it. Pushing through several stacks of mail, she came across a stack that held promise. On the top sat a phone bill and a credit card bill. The third envelope down had a Lions Club return address. Lily picked it up, *eureka,* then wondered what to do with it. She couldn't open it and pull out the fake flyer. Winston would certainly consider that unusual. If she simply moved the envelope to the top of this particular pile, instead of deeper down, that wouldn't guarantee that he'd notice it, much less open it.

Holding the envelope, she mentally worked the problem. An idea came to her and as she developed it, she assigned it a 50/50 chance of success. Well, better than nothing. Such was the risk of a covert matchmaker.

Knowing her time was limited, she rolled up her sleeves went to work.

• • • •

WINSTON HUSTLED REBEL through their nightly walk, his stomach growling in anticipation of his mom's spaghetti pie. It was a simple recipe, and he had made it for himself on occasion, but the thought of digging into its pasta goodness in a few short minutes made him happy. It was a recipe that all the women in his family made for large groups – his grandma, his aunt, his mom. It was a family favorite, and it never disappointed.

Arriving back home, he let himself and Rebel in, went straight to the kitchen where he poured Rebel's dog food into her big metal bowl and breathed in deep. Sure smelled good in here. He turned to the doorway into the dining room and noticed an amazing transformation. Not only had his mom cleared the table of its normal debris, she'd set the table with plates and silverware, the steaming casserole in its place of honor in the center.

"Hungry?" Mom asked. Instead of answering he gave her a meaningful look. "I know, you're always hungry," she said with a laugh.

He cut large squares and scooped one onto each plate. "Thanks again, Mom. This smells so good."

"Couldn't pass up a chance to have a home cooked meal with my favorite son."

With a mouthful, he gave her a thumbs up and spent the next ten minutes eating without conversation. Finishing his first piece, he helped himself to a second while his mom continued to eat more slowly. His hunger curbed, they chatted comfortably about his work, her activities, and future family gatherings.

When they'd both had enough, they leaned back in their chairs, content. Mom said, "Sweetie, I hate to beat a dead horse."

"I know."

"And I hate to sully a great meal."

Winston stood and gathered both plates. "No way you could sully that meal, Mom. That was delicious."

His mom gave the expression she always did when he complimented her as she was trying to discipline him. "Thank you. But Winston, honestly. This place is a wretched mess. How on earth can you live like this?"

He turned his back and carried the load to the sink. Instead of simply dumping them in like he normally would, he humored her and took the trouble to place them in the dishwasher. "I know, Mom. It's messy, but honestly, who cares? I don't, and Rebel certainly doesn't."

She joined him in the kitchen. They worked together to place the remaining slices of pasta into storage bowls for the refrigerator and wash the casserole dish. "True, but you know it doesn't take that much time to pick up after yourself day by day, then it never gets this bad."

He knew she was right. Staring at a big mess and thinking of cleaning it was tiring, and he was more likely to ignore it than dig into it. "I rarely have visitors. When I do it's you, or you and Dad. And you guys love me despite my mess, right?"

Mom tried a different tact. "This is such a cute little cottage, and you're such a successful young man to own a home at such a young age. Why not keep it clean and attractive?"

He shrugged. "I take good care of the place. I've replaced the windows, upgraded the kitchen floor. Painted all the walls. All the long-term stuff that affects resale value. The fact that I don't keep it spotless inside doesn't really bother me. For one thing, I'm busy. And for another thing, I live alone. I don't have to please anyone but myself."

They finished their work in the kitchen and walked into the living room. In his mind, he was berating himself because he'd opened the door with his comments. *That* door that Mom liked to dwell on whenever possible ... his chronic singlehood. He braced himself for what was coming and reminded himself she only wanted him to be happy.

He settled into the couch, Rebel leaping up beside him, curling and plopping down. Mom chose the recliner on the side wall, lifting a sweatshirt that was lying there between her thumb and index finger and looked around, no doubt wondering where to place it. He shrugged. She frowned and draped it over a dining room chair, then sat.

"I think you're missing the big picture, son. You say you live in a pigsty because nobody's ever here but you. But maybe nobody's ever here because your place is such a pigsty."

He let out a chortle, then saw from her expression that she was serious. Hmmm. She'd never used that line of thought before. "I'll take it under advisement, Mom."

But she wasn't going to let it drop. "Are you lonely, son? Are you content without a woman in your life? Do you see yourself having a wife and a family someday?"

The atmosphere in the little room grew heavy. He hated, absolutely hated, disappointing his parents. He'd always worked hard to do the right things, to grow up the way they'd raised him, learn the lessons they'd taught him. And for the most part, he had. But the fact that he was a slob without a girlfriend weighed heavily on his mom's heart, giving her the strong urge to "fix him."

"Let's see," he answered, trying to answer her questions in order. "I am *not* lonely. I have Rebel and all my co-workers and friends. I *am* content without a woman in my life at the moment. And yes, I see myself having a wife and family *someday*. Definitely."

She nodded, evidently satisfied with his answers. "Have you been dating anyone recently?"

"No, Mom."

"So how do you think you're going to get married someday if you don't date?" She huffed out a frustrated breath. "I'm sorry to be so blunt, honey, but you're nearly thirty. It's time to change your dating habits, don't you think?"

"Nearly thirty? Not yet! I'm barely twenty-eight," he protested. "And Mom, I firmly believe that when the right woman comes along, I'll know it." He walked to her chair, took her hand and squeezed it. "I'm happy, Mom. I'm perfectly content with my life. Okay? You don't need to worry about me."

She sighed. "I will always want the best for you. You know that, don't you?"

"I do." He pulled her onto her feet and into a hug. "And thank you for your concern, but really. I'm fine."

She sat back down and studied his face. "You know your dad and I are very proud of you, don't you? All your accomplishments? The man you've become?"

"Yes, Mom, I know." It was a steady in his life. He'd always known just exactly how much he was loved by his parents.

His mother gave him a grim smile. "Okay, changing the subject now."

"Thank God," he mumbled.

"Before I leave, I want to show you something. Shall we?" He followed her back into the dining room where she had placed piles of mail on his sideboard table. She pointed at them. "I couldn't help but notice the mess on your table caused by your daily mail. I want to share a system that I think will work for you so you can be more organized."

He knew he needed to improve in this area so he paid attention while she showed him her system based on due dates of bills so he'd never miss a deadline and pay a late fee. Non-bills lay in a separate pile and she recommended not even letting them gather. Take five minutes every day to open them all and make a decision on the spot whether to throw away or save. Ninety percent would be thrown away, she estimated. That would cut down on clutter and distraction from the important mail.

He nodded. "I understand. Yeah, that looks good, Mom. Thanks, it makes sense."

She gestured to the non-bill pile she'd formed and said, "Let's sample for a minute. Go ahead and open the first few in that pile."

He stifled an eye roll and did as she said. He opened the first envelope. "Looks like a solicitation for a car warranty." He looked at her. "Junk mail."

She gave a thumbs-up. "Pitch."

He opened the next one. "This one looks like junk too."

He started to place it on top of the other, but his mom said, "What is it?"

He turned his attention to it again. "The Lions Club is sponsoring a night at the dog park," he read. "Free treats for the dogs, coffee and appetizers for the humans, a sweepstakes for a free weekend of boarding." He looked up at her, shrugged.

"That sounds fun! When is it?" Mom looked awfully enthused about the event.

He glanced back at the flyer. "Tuesday evening."

She smiled. "Are you free that night?"

"Yeah, I guess."

"You should go! So, attach the flyer to your fridge and write the date on your calendar so you don't forget."

He wasn't so sure he wanted to drag himself out on a work night after he'd just returned from a day at the office, but for the sake of Mom's organization demonstration, he nodded. "Okay, got it."

"Do you think you'll go?" Mom pressed. "I bet Rebel would have a great time."

"Yeah, she probably would. I haven't taken her to a dog park in a while." But the truth was, he loved his evening routine just as much as Rebel did. Drive home from work, walk with

Rebel, eat, and game. Throwing a monkey wrench into that routine made him feel itchy.

His mother seemed satisfied that he was adequately oriented on her household organization system. She picked up the clean casserole dish and gave him a kiss on the cheek. "My work here is done. Great to see you, sweetie."

He walked her to the door. "See you soon, Mom. Thanks again for the dinner." With a wave, she left. He walked into the living room and fired up his gaming system.

• • • •

IN THE CAR, LILY CHOSE Rose's number in her phone's contacts and placed the call. When Rose answered she said, "I've done the best I can without him getting suspicious. He's seen the invitation and has that night free."

Rose's shrills of excitement filled the connection. They chatted for a few moments and Lily ended the call. Thinking it couldn't hurt, she directed a quick prayer for assistance to the heavens.

Chapter Six: An Outing for Winston

Matchmaking Moms of Oceanview Church

"WANNA TAKE A BREAK?"

The sound floated in the air, sort of like a mosquito in his ear. He was aware of it, but he wasn't paying attention.

"Hey! Winston!"

His head jerked up. "Huh?"

It was Vanessa, his work buddy. She shook her empty coffee mug in his face. "Coffee break?"

He shook his head. "Yeah, I guess." He stood up.

"After all those flowcharts you were studying with such intense concentration, your eyes need a break." She took off down the aisle and he followed her.

His brain needed some down time too, judging from the headache pricking his right lobe. He shook his head again to clear it as he walked. They arrived at the break area in their quadrant of the building, a casual room containing tables and chairs, and a few comfy armchairs along the wall. Coffee sat in tall metal decanters, available for free, or the fancier flavored types were available for sale by cup in the vending machine. Winston chose the free stuff and so did Vanessa.

Cups full, they chose an empty table and sat down. "So how are your accounts going?" Vanessa asked.

"Good. A little crazy. They all want to hit new output goals with the new year, and they want my help getting all their supplies lined up." He took a gulp and savored the warmth spreading through his body.

"Really? You must have the overachiever accounts. Mine are content with last year's goals. Fine by me." She laughed and took a sip, followed by a look of disgust. "Ugh. Why do we drink this stuff?"

Winston shrugged. "Because it's free. Would you rather pay three fifty for a cup of that stuff?" He pointed at the machine.

"No," she mumbled. "I really need to get up fifteen minutes earlier in the morning and make my own to bring in."

He nodded. "So how are John and Gracie?" he asked, inquiring about her husband and two-year-old daughter.

He'd met them several times. John was just as outgoing and friendly as Vanessa, and their daughter was the center of their world, although adjusting to working dual-parenthood had not been easy. Listening to his "work wife" discuss her family life, so different from his, enforced his suspicions that if he were ever blessed with a wife and a family, it would be completely awesome to have one parent home with the baby until said baby was in school. Whether that meant a stay-at-home mom, him quitting his job for a few years to take care of the baby, he and his wife working different shifts so one of them was always at home, or at the very least, one of them with a flexible work-from-home arrangement so the baby was always in view. Two parents working full-time away from home while the child is in daycare was the way he grew up. He'd survived, sure, and so had lots of other kids in the same boat, but he'd heard more and more from his generational contemporaries that they wanted a different sort of upbringing for their own families. Less work-oriented, more family-oriented.

Vanessa finished her diatribe about the two most important people in her life and turned to him. "How's Rebel?"

He let out a chuckle. "She's good."

"Anything else new in your life?" she asked.

"Not really."

She shook her head. "You're hopeless."

He groaned. "Don't start...."

She laughed. "Has your mother been nagging you lately?"

"Just this week, in fact."

She patted his hand. "We both just want the best for you."

"I realize that. But why are you two more interested in my love life than I am?" He gave her a cross-eyed look.

"Because we've both found the person who makes us whole. We both know how good a great relationship can be. And we want the same for you."

He pressed his lips together in a line.

"You are a great guy, and you'd make a great boyfriend, husband and father. But for some reason you can't get off your butt and find someone to date. It's a numbers game. The more girls you ask out, the more likely one will say yes. The more girls you date, the more likely you'll find the one who's perfect for you."

He rolled his eyes. "Stop."

"Okay. Topic closed."

"Thank you." He drank another mouthful of rotgut coffee, pulled his phone out of his pocket and checked the time. "I should probably get back."

"Five more minutes, workaholic." She smiled at him. "Anything on the schedule for tonight?"

He shook his head, then paused as he remembered. "Possibly a dog park outing, if I feel like it."

"Oh, what's that?"

"Some organized outing for dog owners and their dogs at the park."

"That might be fun."

He nodded. "Yeah, it's probably good to know more people with dogs so I could socialize Rebel a little more."

"You should go," Vanessa nodded encouragingly.

"I'll see how I feel by the time it starts. Rebel would probably enjoy it. We'll see."

She gave him an amused frown. "You're so decisive."

"Hey, I'm crazy busy all day at work. I like to take the opposite approach at home."

"Yeah," she said longingly. "I personally don't have the option to be relaxed at home, but I can see how that would be pleasant."

He smiled and stood. "Back to work for me, bud."

She waved tiredly and he went back to his desk.

• • • •

WINSTON ARRIVED AT home after work. The idea of the possible dog park outing later that evening on his mind, he shortened Rebel's walk and fed her on their return. He popped a leftover slice of spaghetti pie in the microwave for dinner, then fired up his gaming system. He was leaning toward heading over to the dog park in a few hours, a nice treat for Rebel, so maybe he could play an early game before he left.

His handle was out there in the webs, hovering, an hour or so earlier than his normal routine. Winston hoped it enticed some players to come join him. He sat quietly, waiting. None of the familiar players that normally joined him later in the evening were online yet. But he had cast his net. Now he'd just wait and see if he caught anything.

Focusing on the paused game screen, his mind wandered to the one handle he hoped he'd see this afternoon. He wondered what LeiaPower was doing. Where she was doing it. What she looked like. Was she nice? Was she pretty?

He focused on remembering her voice. Deep and low for a woman, confident, a hint of humor lacing its edges. Judging only from the sound of her voice, he'd guess she was attractive.

He sniffed. He'd never, ever crossed the line and found out anything personal about his online gaming partners. He'd been playing regularly for close to a decade and he'd never thought it a good idea. He'd kept their worlds separate. What he did all day, where he lived, was personal. What he did online was pretend. It was play.

On the other hand, he'd never encountered a female gamer before. Was that the difference? Was that why he was sort of hooked on LeiaPower, thinking of her in the off hours when he was in his real world? Because she was a novelty in the male-dominated world of online gaming? She made him curious, that was for sure.

He didn't know the protocol here. Well, yes he did. The protocol would be to just treat her like any other gaming partner. He had over two dozen of them. Treat her the same way he did them. Compete against them, chat with them occasionally, move on.

A bubble popped onto his screen, someone who wanted to join his game. In spite of himself, he gasped.

It was LeiaPower. She was online and ready to play.

His fingers trembled as he reached for his headphones. Just as he slipped them over his ears she greeted him with that voice he'd been thinking about: "Hey Win4U. You're on early."

His lips curled up. She knew his schedule? Did that mean, dare he hope, that she'd been checking him out too?

"Yes. You wanna play?" He kept it casual.

"Sure thing."

Smiling with pleasure, he started the game and off they went. After an hour, LeiaPower was slightly ahead. Was he distracted and off his game? Or was she truly competitive, her skills close to his?

She paused the game and said, "Sorry, I gotta go. See you next time?"

"Noooooo," he protested. "You can't leave me hanging!"

"Ha ha," came her response. "I'm late for work already."

He paused. He was about to cross a line and wasn't sure if he should. He put his hands in his lap. Of course he shouldn't. He knew the unwritten rules of online game play. Don't get personal with your game mates. Keep it anonymous.

And yet ... "What do you do for work?" he asked casually. It wasn't that personal, as personal questions go. It wasn't like he'd asked her name or where she lived. Whatever her answer was, could apply to thousands of other people.

"I'm the night shift manager at a hotel."

Relief flooded his heart. Because she'd responded. Because she wasn't disturbed by the ill-advised question. And because she had a respectable job.

Maybe she was a respectable girl?

"Have a good night."

"You too, Win4U."

The exchange made him smile.

• • • •

NINETY MINUTES LATER, he was still in an exceptional mood. Why not get out in the beautiful Lowcountry January temps and do something a little different? Go meet some other dog people and let Rebel socialize a little bit? He grabbed her harness and leash and wrestled it on her. "Want to go play?" he asked. Off they went to the car.

A short drive later, he arrived at the dog park listed on the flyer. They'd been here before, on occasion. Beautifully maintained, it contained a large patch of fenced-in yard, lots of trees that provided shade and a carpet of pine needles and leaves. The first thing he noticed was ... nothing. No one was here. No crowd, no organizers, no food. Not a single dog. He grabbed the flyer he'd tossed on the front seat. He double-checked the place and the time. He had not messed up. This was the correct date, time and place.

So why was there no one here?

Rebel whined in the backseat. "Okay, sorry, girl. We'll get out." Regardless of whether anyone else came, she'd still have fun running around off-leash and sniffing. He came around and opened her door. She jumped to the ground, shook her whole body and wagged her tail. He led her to the chain link gate and opened it. She trotted in. He removed her leash. "There you go, girl. Have fun."

He wondered if there was someone to call. He'd left the flyer in the car but he didn't recall a phone number on it. Maybe they'd changed the date or cancelled, and everyone got word except him? Maybe they'd asked for an RSVP and he'd ignored that direction since he'd spontaneously decided to attend.

Didn't matter. He was here, Rebel was here, he was in a great mood from his silly little exchange with LeiaPower. Life was good.

Five minutes later, another car pulled into the parking lot. He glanced over. A good-looking woman roughly his age emerged from the car. She was petite, long brown hair pulled up in a ponytail, and she wore yoga pants and a hot pink shirt. She opened the back door and pulled out a majestic German Shepherd, speaking happily to him. She glanced up and around the parking lot. The confused expression on her face no doubt meant she was noticing as he had that the event was severely under attended. He held up a hand. She waved and led the dog to the gate.

"Hi," she called as she approached. He made his way quickly to the gate to help her open it while she held onto the big dog. "Oh, thanks, that's kind of you."

"Hi, no problem," he said as the girl and her dog entered the yard. She removed the leash and the shepherd scampered off. "My dog's friendly," he said as he pointed to Rebel who was sniffing on the far fence. "That's Rebel."

"Oh, my gosh, she's beautiful!" the girl said enthusiastically. "Max is friendly too."

Winston nodded and gazed after the dogs. Max had made his way towards Rebel and they were sniffing noses. "Were you here for the Lions Club outing, by any chance?"

Her eyes opened wide. "Yes! You too? Where is everybody?"

"I have no idea. I thought maybe I'd missed the cancellation or something."

"Well, if you did, then I did too." She looked around. "I'm bummed. I was actually looking forward to a cup of hot chocolate." She pointed a beautiful smile at him.

His heart skipped. Like, it actually jumped and tripped over a beat. He raised a hand and patted his chest. Was it because of her smile, or was he about to need an ambulance?

She held out a hand. "I'm Tina, by the way."

"Winston," he managed to say. "Nice to meet you."

She glanced out at the dogs. They were running side by side, occasionally locking jaws around the other's neck or ear. "Looks like our dogs are fast friends."

He nodded. "Isn't it funny how dogs play? Wrapping their mouths around the neck, pulling on the ears, running into each other?"

Tina let out a cheerful laugh which warmed his heart. "Exactly. They're very physical and very oral. Like a constant wrestling match. As long as they're still wagging tails and not yipping, they're usually having fun."

They both gazed out over the long yard and confirmed that the yellow lab and the German Shepherd seemed to indeed be having fun, prancing, pushing into each other and chasing the other. Winston pointed at a nearby picnic table. "Care to sit?"

"Sure."

They climbed onto the wooden seat, sitting on the tabletop where they could keep a better eye on their dogs. The air was a crisp sixty degrees with little wind.

She sat near him and he was intensely aware of it. He drew a deep breath. Her scent floated on the air, and her closeness made it easy to breathe it in. Fruity, he decided.

"Isn't it crazy that we're the only two here?" she asked.

"Yeah, sure is." Actually, he couldn't help but feel happy about the way the evening had turned out. *Let's review*, he thought. How many evenings in his life had he not only gotten to flirt online with an intriguing new gaming partner, but also sit beside a beautiful fellow dog lover during a calm Lowcountry evening? All in all, this was turning out to be a night to remember.

"How old is Max?" he asked, wanting to talk to her and figuring that a safe topic would be dogs.

"He's four," she said and launched into a story about how she'd adopted him from a shelter when he was just short of his first birthday, a scrawny stray pulled off the streets by Animal Control and delivered to the shelter for rescue. Within three weeks, he'd been bathed, fed, groomed and neutered, and ready for his forever home with Tina when she came looking. She'd always wanted a German Shepherd and felt lucky that she'd found one who needed a home. Despite his age, he'd never received a stitch of training, so she'd dived in immediately and worked on housetraining, then basic obedience. "It was some work, but you know what? I wouldn't change a thing. I love him to death and can't imagine life without him."

Winston nodded. "I know exactly what you mean. I took a different path acquiring Rebel but same outcome. An Amish farm was advertising purebred lab pups. I drove about two hours to get there, and the farm was immaculate. A teenager was handling the sale and he led me into the barn. We walked past several stalls containing these huge majestic horses."

"Work horses, probably," she said.

"Yes. The Amish don't really keep pets. Everybody has a job." He glanced at her. Her eyes danced. She loved animals, it was clear, and talking about them made her animated. "The kid pulled open a stall door and out tumbled a pile of puppies. Black, yellow, chocolate, the litter had all the colors."

"Oh, my gosh!" she laughed. "I can just picture them. Piles of puppies."

He smiled, gratified at her response.

"How did you choose one?" she asked with a happy smile.

"I sat down in the aisle and they all climbed up on me. I looked at each one and I ended up picking the one who seemed to be the most interested in me. I knew she was the one."

"Was she a tiny puppy?"

He nodded. "Sure was. She was like eight pounds. And now she's eighty-eight. Amazing transformation." Of course, he'd been through all the training milestones as well, but Rebel had been pretty good about housetraining, catching on fast. And he should probably be more disciplined about obedience training. He'd taught her enough to sit on command and wait for him to catch up on a walk before stepping off the curb to the street. There were lots more commands he could teach her. He just hadn't gotten around to it.

"And you love her." It was a simple statement and she meant it sincerely. But it caused a strong reaction in him.

She took his breath away.

Chapter Seven: One Magical Evening

THE DOGS RAN, WRESTLED, sniffed and barked. Finally, they were lying in the grass, their sides heaving with exertion.

"I can guess who's going to sleep well tonight."

Tina's giggle was musical. "Max will, definitely. This has been great exercise for him, in addition to the socialization."

"Despite the fail of the formal event, I'd say this was a success for our two dogs." *And for us.* Winston smiled.

"Definitely. They would make good playdate partners," she said.

He nodded in agreement, then blinked. He looked down at the table, realization dawning in his mind like a coastal sunrise. She'd lobbed him an easy pitch. Now it was up to him to swing. He was out of practice at the whole female/male dynamic, but he suspected it wasn't going to get any easier than this.

Pulse racing, he cleared his throat. "Hey, I have an idea. Would you want to exchange phone numbers and keep in touch about getting the dogs together occasionally?"

Her response was immediate. She reached into her pants pocket, pulled out a phone and said, "Great idea! What's your number?"

He rattled off his numbers while she typed them into her phone. A second later, his own phone buzzed. She'd sent him a text.

Eureka. He had Tina's phone number.

Not wanting to make the moment awkward, he came up with another topic to chat about. Not that it was hard. Tina was very easy to talk to. She'd shared many interesting stories and warmed easily to whatever they talked about.

"What do you do, Tina? Work? Go to school?" he ventured.

"I work in a veterinarian's office," she replied. "I love it. I get to spend my days with our furry friends. But I'm considering going back to school to see if I can be a vet myself."

"Wow, that's awesome. Good luck."

"What do you do?" she asked.

He paused. She caught his hesitation. "You can't talk about it? Undercover cop? Underwear model?"

His laugh was sudden and unexpected. "No, no, nothing like that. I work in manufacturing and I could talk your ear off about my job, but most people get that glazed over look in their eye and really regret asking me. I'd hate to do that to you." *Because your eyes are beautiful just the way they are, and I wouldn't want to do anything to change them.*

"Okay. You like it though?"

"Yes, I sure do. I really like the job. I guess a condensed version is I expedite the receipt of parts needed on manufacturing assembly lines."

"All right. Yeah, sounds very technical and specific to that profession. But I can see how it would be important."

"My role keeps costs down, so our results are closely watched."

They talked a little more, covering details about her job with the animals, and then they moved into favorite vacations they'd each taken. Tina suddenly said, "Would you mind if I left Max with you for a few minutes?"

"No, not at all. What ...?"

She climbed off the picnic table and hit the ground running. "I'll be right back!"

He watched her curiously as she ran across the yard, got into her car and drove off. He frowned. That was odd. He turned back to the dogs. She wouldn't leave her dog. She had to be coming back.

He hoped.

In the quiet of the next ten minutes, his mind ran over their conversation. She was fun and happy and positive. Yes, she was beautiful and if given the chance, he'd love to get to know her better. But if all the two of them got together was this evening, he'd call it a success.

His mind ran over his past failures asking females out. None of his past attempts had been as easy, as natural, as the last few hours had been. He realized he hadn't asked her on a date. Her surrendering over her phone number was because of the dogs. And yet ...

Maybe Tina would be the female to break his run of rejections?

Her car returned to the parking lot and she got out. She made her way toward him, holding a lidded cup in each hand. He got up and jogged over to the gate, opening it for her. She beamed at him. "Just because the Lions Club didn't show up with hot chocolate, doesn't mean I had to go without." She handed him one. "I got one for you too."

"Thanks." He took it and let it warm his hand. They climbed back up on the picnic table and sipped their hot drinks. The evening was growing darker and Winston noticed with a fallen heart that the park didn't have lights. As the darkness fell, he could barely see the dogs anymore. He could only judge their presence based on sound and movement.

Normally he'd call Rebel and take her home. But, looking at Tina, he didn't want to. He didn't want the evening to end. It felt like it had a little bit of magic dust sprinkled over it.

He must've chuckled at the image because Tina looked at him. "What?" she asked, ready to laugh too.

He shook his head. "I was just thinking it's so dark I can barely see the dogs anymore. But I don't necessarily want to leave." He would *not* say anything about magic dust. Definitely not.

She nodded. "I know. I feel the same way. On both counts." She rose and tossed her empty cup into a trash bin. Facing him, she held out a hand to shake. "It was nice to meet you, Winston. I've enjoyed chatting with you tonight."

Winston fumbled to his feet. "Yes. Um, me too. I've enjoyed it too."

Another beaming smile and she turned and called her dog. Max lifted his head and bounded to her. Rebel followed him. They harnessed their dogs and walked together to the gate.

Okay, so there it was: the doubt that always plagued him whenever a woman moved from friend status to potential date status. His fear of making a misstep paralyzed him, making him unable to make the transition.

He made his way to his car, getting Rebel settled inside. Closing the door behind her, he turned to face Tina who lingered nearby. He had no idea what to say.

"My next day off is Sunday. Would you have any free time to meet Max and me here?"

Relief swept through him. God bless Tina. She'd saved him. True, it was a doggie playdate. It didn't mean she was interested in him romantically. And that was okay. She'd initiated their second get together.

He'd take it from there for their third. Somehow, between now and then, he'd work up the confidence to ask her on a date.

Or, at least a cup of coffee without the dogs.

Exuberant, he responded, "Anytime. You tell me."

"Four o'clock?" she asked.

"You got it. See you and Max right here, Sunday at four o'clock." His smile was probably way too happy and way too big for the occasion but he couldn't help it. He was seeing Tina again.

Chapter Eight: A Question From Leia

TO WINSTON'S AMUSEMENT, life had taken on a new hue. His mood was brighter. Less things irritated him. Vanessa's teasing jabs bothered him less.

During spare moments when his mind wasn't occupied, his thoughts drifted to Tina. Wondering what she was doing. How she was doing. What she was thinking of. Was she thinking of him, as he was of her?

Being inexperienced as he was with the opposite sex, he had no idea if this was how other guys felt when they met someone special. Maybe Tina didn't share his feelings at all. Maybe she just considered him a guy with a dog that her dog could play with.

But to him, it felt special. And he was interested in seeing if he could take it any further.

His natural inclination to protect his heart from rejection seemed to be fading ... slightly. He was more optimistic this time around.

His childhood was riddled with occasions when he was anxious and impatient, wanting something. Good things come to those that wait; his mother had always told him. It seemed to be good advice right now.

He didn't want to blow it. He didn't want to come on too strong. He didn't want to assume too much.

He needed advice.

He arrived at his desk the morning after the dog park date and for once, he looked forward to Vanessa's daily visit, to their daily break. Vanessa was the perfect one to approach with his questions.

Later that morning, she stopped by and he immediately logged out and rose. "I need your help," he said and breezed toward the break room, barely waiting for her.

"Oh my goodness," she muttered as she trailed behind him.

Their coffees poured, they sat at a table. "So what's up?" she asked with a frown, his change in behavior obvious.

"Remember that dog park outing I mentioned?"

She nodded.

"I went. And I ..." he hadn't formed this particular combination of words in longer than he could remember. "I met someone. A woman."

Vanessa whooped and pumped a fist. He shushed her, embarrassed, glancing around at coworkers who were staring. "Shhhh," he urged.

"Sorry," she whispered, her smile not yet dimmed. "This is great news!"

He let a quiet laugh slip out. "Okay, okay." He looked into his friend's excited face. She was happy for him. After the many times she'd harassed him about his lack of love life, he had to share this tiny step forward with her.

"Tell me."

Winston shared an overview of their evening over the next six or seven minutes, enduring Vanessa's squeals and groans. He finished with the news of their upcoming plans on Sunday.

"Sounds good, Romeo. I don't know why you need my help."

Without realizing it, he was squeezing his hands together. He pulled them apart and sat on them. "I don't know. What if she just thinks of me as a new friend with a dog? What if my feelings for her as a potential romance are unreturned?"

She nodded as she considered his words. "Right. Okay, here's what you do. Take it slow. Don't assume she likes you *like that* until you've spent more time with her. Talk to her more. Listen for clues." She laid her hands flat on the table and went on. "Ninety nine percent of the time, you can't go wrong with a woman taking it slow. Let things develop. Don't rush."

Her words were like a salve on his nerves. Going slow, he could do. If she'd told him to be aggressive and fast, he would've been worried. But slow. Good. He was in no rush. And he didn't want this potential relationship to end up a major failure.

"Okay, good. Be friendly. Don't assume her feelings. Take it slow. I can do that." He checked his watch and tapped it. "Better get back. But Ness, thank you. I mean it."

She gave him a happy grin. "My pleasure. Keep me posted."

• • • •

HIS JUBILANT MOOD LASTED all day, through several meetings, a dozen phone calls and all the way home. He whistled a tune through his walk with Rebel, fed her when they got home, ate his own meal, and powered up his game.

He waited and watched as his normal team joined him online for their evening battle. LookyCookie logged on, RobotSam, WillIAm, and several more. He greeted them through his headphones.

A voice caught him by surprise. "Hello Win4U. How's it going tonight?"

His body responded to her voice, his breath leaving his lungs. *Pull it together*, he told himself. "LeiaPower, hi. It's going great. How about you?"

"Things are good," her soft voice said. "In fact, I have something to talk to you about, off-game. Can you hang on when we're done?"

He blinked, his mouth open. What was this about? His hesitation was stretching, becoming apparent. He needed to respond. "Okay, yeah, sure."

They kicked off the game and he struggled to direct his mind on the challenges at hand. He was Win4U, after all, and had a reputation to uphold. He counted down to game time and off they went.

The battle lasted for three hours. His team victorious, he praised everyone who had fought and displayed bravery. Their winning streak continued. Considering how distracted he was tonight, he considered them lucky. Good thing everyone else stepped up where his own concentration was lacking.

One by one, his teammates dropped offline. He farewelled them all, thanking them, until only he and one other player remained on the gaming connection: LeiaPower.

He got right to it: "You wanted to speak to me, LeiaPower?"

"Yes, I did."

FINDING LOVE FOR THE LONER   67

For some reason, his adrenaline kicked in.

"Have you ever been to a GamingCon?"

He paused. "Uh no, I haven't. Have you?"

"No, but I want to. However I can't afford to go on my own as a guest. So I started thinking about ways that I could go as a workshop leader."

"Oh?" Her voice wrapped itself around his consciousness. What was it about her voice that always got to him?

"Yeah, the deadline to submit workshop applications is coming up in a month. I've been working on a topic that might be approved."

He pulled his attention away from the way her voice muddled his brain and concentrated on what she was telling him. "Okay ..."

"I've done a lot of research, and I think I have a topic." She paused, then said, "You."

"Me!" he snorted.

"Yes. Did you realize you are Star Battler's longest standing victorious captain? No one has won more games than you. No one has been at it as long as you."

He frowned. No, he didn't know that. And he didn't know exactly how to interpret those facts (if they were, in fact, accurate). Was that something to be proud of? Or embarrassed by?

"Win4U?"

Her voice brought him back. "Oh, sorry." He took a breath and cleared his throat. "No. I didn't realize that. Are you sure?"

"Of course! You're a legend of the game. Didn't I tell you that I had to join your team so I could play with the great Win4U? Well, this is why."

He frowned. "Because ...?"

"Because I wanted to play with you, learn from you, and formulate this workshop."

He shook his head, confused. "What is the workshop, exactly?"

"*The Unparalleled Rise of Win4U.*"

Silence flowed through his headphones, pulsating like it was a real thing. He needed to fill it but had no idea what to say. He was speechless. "Excuse me?" he settled for.

She giggled, a flowery sound. "Let me send you my workshop proposal and you can yay or nay it. But do me a favor, please?"

"What?" He pushed the syllable past his breathlessness.

"Read it with an open mind. I've put a lot of work into it, but more than that, I think the gaming world needs to know. I think there will be a lot of interest. And I would love to work together on this with you."

"What?" This conversation had left him unable to say any word other than that one.

She laughed again. "In the proposal, I suggest that the two of us present the workshop together."

"You and me?"

"Yep. I'll present the details about the rise of your fabulous career, then you could do a demonstration on some of your more stellar moves." She laughed. "Pardon the pun."

"Ummm, ..."

"We can't lose. I just know the board would jump on this workshop. And I could attend the conference for free as a workshop leader. But only with your partnership."

She stopped speaking, letting the silence grow between them. His heart raced, uncomfortable with the idea. But what harm could come of reading her proposal? He could figure out what to do once he knew what he was dealing with.

"Okay, send the proposal. I'll take a look."

She squealed, the most emotion he'd ever heard from her. "What's your email address?"

He told her, and they parted.

Chapter Nine: Tina Gets Back in the Saddle

Matchmaking Moms of Oceanview Church

TINA MITCHELL LEFT church with a smile on her face, greeting the friendly faces who had taken her in as one of their own last year. At twenty-five, she'd spent a few years bopping from one church to another as she settled into her new town of Murrells Inlet, South Carolina. When her job as a vet tech brought her here from Atlanta, she knew immediately that she loved it. God's beauty was everywhere she looked. Friendly, happy people. The ocean so close by she could take a walk on its gorgeous shores every day or two. The move had been a good one, just what the doctor ordered for her broken heart and tattered life.

God had played a huge part in that. Emancipating herself from the solid religious upbringing of her childhood, she sampled a new way of living in college. New girlfriends helped her with hair styles and makeup. Wardrobe for her petite figure to accentuate her best features. Parties.

It was fun experimenting at first. After all, she was eighteen, an independent young woman. She could do what she wanted, right? College was a place for a young person to try new things. Like, drinking to excess, staying out late, the occasional entirely regrettable one-night stand. Feeling horribly denigrated in the dim light of morning. Hanging her head with the shame she couldn't help but feel as she made her way to class, hoping that the bad choices she'd made wouldn't brand her.

It was all a lie. She wasn't independent, not really, when it was only by the generosity and love of her parents paying her tuition that she was there. She wasn't there to party and attract boys. She was there to make the most of her opportunity, to finish her education, build skills to start a career.

And painting herself up with makeup and hair and seductive clothes? What was she thinking? Why would she think she would meet a decent man when she presented herself that way? All she got was what she advertised. And that was certainly not what she wanted.

Fortunately, a year into college, God gave her a nudge and a reminder: remember whose you are. You are my child. Now, get going on your real life.

She came away from that year with some solid resolutions: work hard. Get good grades. Stay true to God and her faith. Find a way to be independent for real.

After graduating and moving here, she made it a high priority to look for a church that would be a steady part of her life. She visited church after church in search of just the right place. She knew it when she found her new home. People greeted her like family. The music embedded itself in her soul. The Holy Spirit spoke to her through the sermon and the Bible readings, making her heart sing.

She had settled where she knew God wanted her: Marsh Community Church. As she made her way through the post-service crowd toward the coffee line, she waved at Becky, a friend she'd met at the Singles Group.

"Hey you!" Becky exclaimed. "I didn't see you or I would've sat with you."

"I was a little early and sat up front," Tina said.

"Great sermon, huh?"

"Sure was. Gave me a lot to pray about this week." Tina had admired the pastor's message about not just *telling* people you'd pray for them in times of need, but actually *doing* it. She was guilty of it herself: how many times on social media, or in person, when someone shared some tough times they were going through, she'd said, "Praying for you." Easy to say, but she wasn't quite so strong on the follow through. Pastor's message showed her that words were cheap. In the future, when she said, "I'm praying for you," it was a divine commitment to sit down and follow through. To remember that person, by name, to the Father Almighty.

"Yeah, me, too."

They got in line together and grabbed cups with coffee, then moved to the end to doctor them up with cream. Tina loved how this church went all out and served yummy, delectable coffee, not just the brand in the big can. It was almost like they were proud of their coffee selections and only served the best to their worshippers.

"So what's up today? Any plans?" Becky asked as they settled in an open corner away from the crowd.

"Yes, I have a doggie playdate with a new friend and his dog."

Tina could've sworn she'd said it casually, not encouraging any suspicion, but her friend raised her eyebrows, widened her eyes and said, "A new friend? A *male* new friend? Dish. Now."

Tina laughed and rolled her eyes. "Not much to dish. One of our clients at work invited me to a dog park social earlier this week. I went, but there was a mix-up because there were only two of us there: me and Max, and a guy named Winston and his dog, Rebel." She shrugged. "Anyway, we stayed, and the dogs played, and we talked."

Becky drew her bottom lip between her teeth. "And?"

"And he seemed like a nice guy after two hours of conversation. I suggested another play date today. He said yes."

Becky raised a hand and Tina smacked it, high five. "I like this. Good job."

Tina shrugged. "If nothing else, Max gets a couple play dates with another dog."

"But ... do you think it'll be more than that?"

Tina started to respond, and then paused. "I want to take it a step at a time. I don't want to be boy-crazy, getting all excited about every guy I meet, wanting them to be my next boyfriend. God knows who the right person is for me. I want to follow His will."

Becky stared at her, her excited face softening. Finally, she nodded. "You are absolutely right. I am so impressed with you right now. Have a good time with this dog guy and don't jump in headfirst. Wait for God's guidance. You go, girl."

Tina smiled and their conversation drifted in other directions until she decided to go. She gave her friend a hug.

On her way out to the car, she prayed that God would help her remember her resolve. During her year in college when she went crazy, she'd jumped too quickly into the wrong relationships and gave her heart away too easily. All it caused was pain and heartache. But in her diligence to follow God's will and save herself for the man God had planned for her, she had cut off all dating. She'd gotten into her mind, if she saw one ungodlike flaw, why bother with him? He obviously wasn't the one God had planned for her.

But now, looking at it as a mature woman in her mid-twenties, another truth had been revealed to her. People weren't perfect. She certainly wasn't, and neither were the men she could be dating. God had a history of picking imperfect people to do His will. King Solomon, Joseph, David, the Apostle Paul, Jesus' disciples. None of them were people with the perfect resume to carry out the job God had in store for them. He picked imperfect people, let them struggle, and then helped them through to success.

So, she'd enter this date with Winston with a new plan. She'd been too far to the left, and too far to the right. How about if she met God somewhere in the middle?

She smiled, pleased with where her head was, how God had helped her get there. Winston Adams may be the next big love of her life. Or he may be someone she'd spend exactly one afternoon with and never see again. Only God knew.

But her heart fluttered with anticipation of their afternoon together.

• • • •

THE HANDS OF WINSTON'S old-fashioned clock, hanging on his living room wall, seemed to be moving extra-slow today. He'd gotten up twice to check it out – made sure the batteries were in, compared the time to his cell phone – and it was, indeed, accurate. Why did it seem like the minutes were dragging?

He sat again, trying to concentrate on a movie marathon he was watching on the sci-fi channel. They were playing the Star Wars episodes back to back all weekend. Of course, he'd seen them all, many times, but it never bothered him to see them again.

Rebel walked over and sat, resting her head on his knee. He stroked the soft fur on top of her head and scratched behind her ears. "Hey, babe. You've got a date today with Max. That'll be fun, huh?"

Winston glanced back at the big clock. Two thirty. His mind started wandering to what he could do to make this a memorable, one-of-a-kind day. Something to make him stand out to beautiful Tina. Someone she'd want to spend more time with. They were meeting at four o'clock, so after a few hours they'd both be hungry for dinner. Inviting her out to a restaurant would be impossible because they both had their big dogs with them.

Invite her back here to throw something on the grill? He glanced around and immediately decided against it. He didn't want to admit it, but his mom was probably right. Looking at this place with a fresh eye, he came to the realization: it was a mess. It would take him hours to get it glistening, and he didn't have the time. Besides, his fridge was empty, as usual.

So, what else could he do? Pack a picnic lunch? Again, he had no food, and going shopping and preparing it himself would take more time than he had remaining.

Or, maybe bring some nice sandwiches from the shop on the corner. He'd buy a variety of options, complete with chips and side salads, drinks. She'd have to like something. He'd keep them in a cooler in the trunk and during the date, he'd monitor the situation. If she made it clear she was only interested in him as another dog owner, he wouldn't ask her to stay for dinner. The last thing he wanted was to put himself out there, vulnerable to her imminent rejection.

Bringing a bunch of food could make him look like an idiot, especially if she had no interest whatsoever in him on a personal level.

He sighed. He was right back in the same mental cycle that always materialized when there was a woman he was interested in. Why was this so hard for him?

All his friends were either married or involved with someone special. He was a "normal" guy – educated, self-sufficient, relatively handsome, at least people had told him so. Why did he have such trouble with the fairer gender? It didn't need to be this hard.

He needed an advisor. How he wished for a brother he could run these doubts by without the risk of being ridiculed. It was difficult to bare his soul and admit his shortcomings, even to a buddy.

Then he thought of Vanessa. Even though they were strictly work buddies, he was much more likely to ask her advice than one of his married friends.

He pulled his phone out of his pocket and searched his Contacts. Yep, just as he suspected, he had her number, even though they rarely spoke on the phone. Before talking himself out of it, he placed the call. She answered right away with a greeting.

"Sorry to bug you on a weekend, but I need some advice and I didn't really have anyone else to ask."

"Is this about your date with the hot new woman?"

He made a sound which told her exactly what he thought about that description. "Don't laugh at me but let me run this by you. Tell me honestly what you think. We're meeting at the dog park at four. The dogs'll play for probably an hour or two. When they're done, it's dinner time."

"Ahh, I see where you're going."

"I thought about stopping by the sandwich shop and picking up food and keeping it in my trunk. When we're hungry I could surprise her with it and we could eat it at the park. What do you think?"

"Yes! It shows her that you put some thought into the date, planned ahead, were proactive about her needs. Throw in a vase with a carnation or two and a nice tablecloth."

Winston shook his head. "Okay, no. I don't have either of those things, and the date is now an hour away. Besides, what if she thinks that's, I don't know, over the top?"

"If she likes you, she'll love it."

"Well, that's the problem, isn't it? How do I know if she likes me, versus she just likes my dog?"

Vanessa's laugh carried through the phone. Winston cringed. "You really are a mental case, aren't you? Okay, listen to me. She'll give out clues while you're chatting. If she's friendly and smiles a lot and laughs at your pathetic jokes, then do it. If she sits there, crosses her arms over her chest and reads her phone, then don't do it."

She'd meant it to be funny, but instead it caused a rush of anxiety in his esophagus. "It's not that cut and dry, and you know it."

"I'm sorry. But seriously. It's not a marriage proposal. If you bring out the romantic dinner and she doesn't like it, just tell her, you were hungry and figured she'd be too. No big deal. Then, move on. No harm done."

He was nodding. Maybe he could do this. If she rejected him, so what? No one was watching, and they had no friends in common. It could be his little secret. One more feminine rejection to add to his collection. "Okay, I got it. Thanks."

"Call me later and let me know how it goes," she said in a sing-song voice.

"That's a definite maybe." He broke the connection and got Rebel ready to go.

• • • •

TINA PULLED INTO THE lot of the dog park and glanced over at the yard. Despite herself, her heart jumped a little. Winston was already there, sitting in "their" spot on the top of the picnic table. A grin covered her face, her heart like a rainbow filling her body.

God, she prayed, *don't let me get ahead of myself. If this is a man you want me to spend time with, please make it clear. Don't let me go taking myself down the wrong path. I'm ready for a real relationship with the right guy.*

She pulled Max out of the car and headed for the gate. Winston had spotted her coming, and was approaching the gate with the most beautiful, happy smile she'd ever seen. *Darn it, God, if he's not the one you intend for me, it's going to be hard to pass up that smile.*

She greeted him with her own big smile, the one that naturally sprang to her face. "Hi, Winston!"

He helpfully pulled open the indoor gate so that she could focus on wrangling Max through the outdoor gate. "Hello there," he answered and reached for Max's leash. Eventually they were all inside the yard, gates secured. She removed his leash. "Run and be free, boy," she said and watched the dog run off in search of Rebel.

She let out a big breath. Winston stood right in front of her, looking and smelling good. How did he do that, while standing inside a dusty yard full of animals? "You look nice," she said sweetly.

He went still for a moment, his eyes slightly widened, and he responded with a smile, "Likewise. You look very nice, Tina."

She chuckled. His response was a little awkward, but she'd thrown him for a loop with her initial compliment. She took his arm and walked toward the table. "I saw you reserved our spot."

"Yeah, it seemed to work well the last time we were here."

She climbed up on the tabletop and turned toward him. "So, how's your week been?"

"Great," he said. "Work's been good, I guess. Same old, same old, but no big problems."

She noticed that he shook his head, as if he wasn't pleased with his answer. Her heart overflowed with affection for him. He was shy, she guessed. Although why he would be, she couldn't imagine. He was accomplished, friendly, attractive. Maybe he was just shy around women he liked?

Her heart surged. Did he like her? Was he interested in her? If so, that made her happy. She just needed the green light from God.

To give him a break, she launched into a story from work. She had a million of them. Working with animals gave her an endless supply of funny stories. The fact that they both loved dogs gave her material to fill the time with conversation and laughs.

Time passed quickly. The dogs got along great, chasing each other, sniffing in the corners, wrestling without getting too rough. And she and Winston got along great too. He'd laughed at her stories, he'd told a few of his own, and the minutes had flown.

A loud growl emitted from her stomach and she instantly covered it with her hands. "Oh, my gosh!" she laughed. "I guess someone thinks it's dinnertime!"

"Are you hungry?" he asked with a smile.

"I would say so!"

He held up an index finger. "Wait right here. Can you keep an eye on both dogs for a few minutes?"

She nodded with a grin, curious about what would happen next.

He jumped down from the table and jogged out of the yard, to his car. She watched while he pulled a cooler out of his trunk and draped a large cloth or blanket over his arm. *My gosh, he had food!*

As he walked back, arms loaded with the cooler, she joined him at the gate and opened it. "What is this? Do you have food in there?" she asked excitedly.

He laughed but didn't answer. He set the cooler on the ground and tossed what Tina now saw was a tablecloth, over the picnic table. She straightened out the edges while he opened the cooler. The first thing he pulled out was a bud vase containing two white carnations.

She gasped, her hands over her mouth. "You brought a centerpiece?"

His gaze paused on her face and he answered slowly, "Y-y-y-es?"

"So cool!" she assured him. He nodded, then dug back into the cooler, bringing out white paper bags. He set them on the covered table and reached in, pulling out wrapped sandwiches. By now, the dogs had smelled the aroma and had run over to join them.

"You are a godsend!" Tina exclaimed. She reached for the half dozen sandwiches and read the labels on the wrappers: "Ham and swiss, turkey and cheddar, tuna salad, roast beef. Winston, how did you know all my favorites?"

"I just got a variety. I hoped I'd hit on something that you liked."

She quieted, and for some inexplicable reason, tears threatened her eyes. She rubbed them before tears dropped. "This is so sweet, thank you. I love this."

He didn't answer right away, instead, gazed closely at her. His eyebrows dropped momentarily. "You're welcome. I figured we'd be hungry eventually, but we'd have the dogs with us so we couldn't really go out."

"You're so thoughtful." Her voice cracked, but she hoped he didn't catch it. Or maybe he'd just think it was normal for her voice to crack at the slightest bit of kindness shown her by a man. Because in her dating history, she couldn't quickly come up with a memory of a guy being this considerate and thoughtful. Of course, she'd dated quite a lot of losers up to this point.

She caught her breath. She'd been asking God for a winner, and this was the response. She didn't need to be hit over the head. She recognized answered prayer when she saw it.

"Thank you," she whispered. Now she just needed to calm down and not scare the poor guy away.

Chapter Ten: Leia Makes Her Move

"WELL?"

Winston had expected a visit from Vanessa, and here she was. Ten minutes into the workday. The woman had nothing if not restraint. He kept his head down, determined not to meet eyes with her. After all, most guys his age, after having a successful first dinner with a new woman, wouldn't be dishing all the details to a work buddy the next day.

Would they?

His attempt to appear mature and nonchalant backfired on him when she repeated, "Well? Well? Well?" His lip curled up and he couldn't help the chuckle that escaped.

He looked up at her. Instead of speaking, he gave her a thumbs-up.

"I knew it!" she exclaimed, then looked around, darted into his cube and sat in his side chair. In a quieter voice, she said, "Tell. Me. Everything."

He shrugged. "She liked the dinner idea. It went well."

"And the tablecloth and flowers?"

He nodded. "She specifically praised the centerpiece."

"I knew it!"

"Thanks for bringing those and meeting me at the sandwich shop, by the way. You didn't have to, but I appreciated the support."

She patted his shoulder. "No problem, bud. I got your six, as they say. So, what next?" She frowned and locked her gaze on his face. "I hope you had the sense to ask her out on a proper date without the dogs. Tell me you did. Please tell me."

As much as he wanted to play it cool, Vanessa knew him too well. She was along with him on this journey, and she deserved to know. "I did."

Vanessa let out another whoop. Winston rose from his chair, looking around at his coworkers like a groundhog peeking out of his hole. He lowered himself. "Would you keep it down, please?"

"Okay." Vanessa stood. "Tell me at break time." She held up a palm for him to slap. "Nice work, Romeo."

He waved her away and got back to work.

•   •   •   •

IT WAS AMAZING, WINSTON noted, how pleasant Monday was following his Sunday date with Tina. Sure, he had the same number of production calls and problems and quotas to meet. He had the usual angry vendors to deal with and warehouse superintendents to calm down. But his mindset was peaceful and calm. Happy. Nothing could rattle him.

It had to be because of Tina.

Now, the wondering was over. Did she like him? Yes, he was pretty sure she did. No, he was definitely sure. Their conversation as the dogs played was fun and easy, but when she saw that he'd brought dinner, she'd seemed downright ... amazed.

It was such an easy thing to do, but she acted like it was a monumental feat. She was so grateful, so impressed. He swore he saw tears in her eyes, more than once. He wondered what that was all about. But hey, he didn't pry. It was enough for him to present the meal and see that she appreciated it.

And afterward, she left no doubt in his mind that she liked him. As he was picking up the empty wrappers and cleaning up the table, she came up behind him and touched his arm. Turning into her, she was right there, chin raised, eyes closed.

He didn't remember if he had kissed her, or she had kissed him, but it didn't matter. They met in the middle, both of their minds in unison on one thing: that first kiss. And it was phenomenal.

He put absolutely everything out of his mind except meeting her lips with his own. Hers were soft. And warm. They felt good against his.

When she pulled back from him, they kept their gazes locked. Those dark chocolate eyes and the smile told him, she liked it too. It was a good thing, this first kiss. First of many, maybe.

It had left them both a little breathless. They chuckled and she helped him with the cleanup task. Then it was all about throwing trash away, calling the dogs over, loading them into their cars. He'd made a decision then. Well, two decisions.

He was going to ask her out on a date without the dogs.

And he was going to kiss her goodnight.

He was successful on both counts, and now he had a date on Friday night to look forward to. "Leave it to me," he'd told her. "I'll make the plans."

She'd beamed with approval and said, "Just let me know how to dress."

He'd nodded. That meant he needed to plan the date in time to let her know.

Now, it was Monday evening and he still had that lingering happy feeling. That sense of "I can do anything, accomplish anything. Anything is possible." He wondered if all men felt that way when a date with a special woman went well, and he was just late to the party. Or, was he the only one to feel it?

Or, was Tina the only woman who would make him feel that way?

He shook his head while he logged on to his game system. Way to get ahead of himself. He'd take it one step at a time and see where it led.

His playing partners joined him online, their tag names popping onto the screen seconds before their voices filled his headphones. He greeted them all.

"Hey Robot. Hi Milers. How's it going Snacky?"

LeiaPower greeted him before he had a chance to. "Hey Captain. How are you tonight?"

Her voice was deep and sultry as usual. He wondered if that was how she sounded in real life or if she had perfected her tone just for online game play. "Hi LeiaPower. I'm great. How about you?"

"Good, also. Could I entice you to stay after class tonight?" Her amusement was evident in her tone. He assumed she was kidding around with him, but he couldn't help feeling a little uncomfortable. First of all, he didn't want his other players to think that he and Leia had a relationship that didn't include them. Something secret and special, because that was not conducive of a strong leader. And besides, it wasn't true. And second, her word choice, *entice you to stay*, made it seem like that's precisely what she was trying to imply.

"Ah yes, you have business to discuss, don't you?" he responded as best he could on short notice, hoping it eliminated any thoughts of impropriety by his eavesdropping teammates.

"Yes, boss."

His strategy backfired on him because of the suggestive way she'd uttered those two words. But greeting time was over. The minutes had ticked down and it was time to play. His team needed him to lead with a full focus. He'd have to put LeiaPower out of his mind.

When the game ended, Winston stayed online while all his teammates dropped off. They had lost their battle tonight but it had been close. They'd all worked hard but sometimes you have to admit defeat. Winston wondered if the defeat had been partially due to his distraction over Leia and their upcoming conversation. He hoped not.

"Win4U. Rough night."

"Yeah."

"You win some, you lose some." She paused and then changed subjects. "I assume you read my workshop proposal, Captain?"

He knew this conversation was coming, and he was dreading it. "Yeah. First of all, you don't have to call me Captain when we're outside the game."

"Win4U then?"

"Or, how about we call each other by our names? I'm Winston."

"Winston," she said as if pulling the sound over her tongue, trying it on for size. "Nice. I'm, as you may have guessed, Leia."

He mumbled an acknowledgement. "Yes, I read the proposal, but if I'm being honest, I have to say it makes me uncomfortable."

"Really? Why?"

He exhaled and scratched his forehead. "I don't how to say this right. Um, it's too complimentary of me."

Her tone was straight. "They're not compliments, Winston, they're facts."

"Are you sure?"

"Of course, I'm sure. I've done my homework on you. Every fact is in the public Star Battler record. Anyone can check their accuracy. Including you."

He shook his head. "Your proposal just makes me sound so ... over the top. Like I think very highly of myself. Like I'm conceited."

She made a little sound; he was unsure if it came from humor or irritation. "You didn't propose the workshop topic. I did. How could that make you seem conceited?"

He hesitated. "I'm sorry. I know you put a lot of hard work into this. And I know you can't go to the conference without having a workshop accepted. But I don't feel comfortable having a workshop presented about ... me."

"It's not about you personally, Winston. It's about your career as Win4U. I can keep the two separate, I promise. This will be all about your gaming prowess, nothing else." She paused. "Does that make you feel any better?"

It did, slightly. But not entirely.

"I tell you what, let me present the first twenty minutes of the workshop to you and you tell me if it makes you feel uncomfortable. I get that you're humble and modest. That probably leads to your success as a great leader. But your career highlights are admirable. You are a legend in our game. I know tons of gamers would want to come to the workshop, hear about you, and meet you. Please?"

A random Bible verse planted itself in his mind. "Humble yourself before the Lord and he will lift you up." And another verse he'd learned from his mother, "When pride comes, then comes disgrace." How could he explain to Leia that letting her boast about him during a workshop was prideful, and it was not what the Bible taught us?

"I don't know."

"Please. Like I told you, I really want to go to GamingCon but this is my only way. I've got to concoct a workshop topic that the committee will jump on. I just have a good feeling that if I submit this, and especially if you are onboard to demonstrate, I can't lose. Please Winston? Do this for me?"

He should have put an end to it. He wasn't sure, thinking about it afterward, why he didn't. Maybe because he didn't want to disappoint her? He didn't want to be the reason that her dream to attend GamingCon would crash and burn? Or was it because he wanted to live up to the crazy high standard she already thought he was?

Regardless, he agreed to meeting through a video call in a few nights' time so she could run through the first part of her workshop. He only hoped he felt comfortable with the content, but he knew, knowing how much it meant to her, it would be very difficult to say no.

Chapter Eleven: A Date Without the Dogs

FRIDAY WAS AN ODD SORT of day for Tina. The morning dragged on forever, making her think she'd never get to the end of it. But after she'd made the arrangement with a co-worker to cover her late afternoon clients so she could leave a few hours early, time shifted into hyper-speed.

She was in the back room, wrestling with a big golden doodle, attempting to calm her and draw a vial of blood, but the patient wasn't cooperating. She hated the idea of tying her down. She'd rather just talk her into calming and get the vial without incident.

Barbara came into the room and threw her a look of confusion. "I thought you were leaving early." She tapped her wristwatch. "You're ten minutes late already."

Tina sighed, a frown on her face. "I know. I thought I could get this blood drawn before I left but Mr. Rufus here is making it difficult."

Barbara came over with a smile and took hold of Rufus' lead. She squatted in front of the big dog and petted his head, shushing him. "There, big guy. You are just a little frightened, aren't you? Nothing to be scared of. No one wants to hurt you."

Tina took advantage of the help and expertly extracted the blood while Rufus was distracted. "Perfect. Thank you!" She pulled a label off the printer, slapped it on the vial and placed it in the rack. "I'll just return this big man to Room 3 and I'll be outta here."

"Got plans tonight?" Barbara asked, stroking Rufus' furry head.

Tina could feel the happy smile on her face that popped there without warning. "A date."

"Oh! Have a great time. And look, get going. I'll take Rufus." She shooed her away and led the big dog out.

"Really? Well, thank you!" Tina exclaimed and shuffled out the door.

An hour later, she'd showered, shaved her legs, washed and conditioned her hair, and she was now soaking in a bath full of moisturized water. She needed to relax after the day on her feet, and the warm bath not only soothed her body but also her mind.

How long had it been since she'd prepared herself for a date with a guy she liked? Too long to count, and even longer getting ready for a guy she liked as much as she liked Winston. Her heart raced when she thought of him, and she got that delicious dash of adrenaline.

She sank further into the water and thought about all his good qualities that made her go dizzy. *Let me count the ways,* she mused with a smile. He was kind. He was good. Thoughtful, selfless. He put her needs above his own. Oh, and he was cute. Handsome, really, but that sweet little grin made him look so youthful that she thought of him as cute. She'd love to run her fingers through that chestnut colored hair, and then, for good measure, down his cheek. He had a wonderful face, a beautiful smile, and mesmerizing blue eyes.

He was easy to talk to. He wasn't stuck-up, as were the good-looking guys she'd encountered in college. He acted interested in what she had to say, even if her conversation wasn't exactly stellar. He never appeared bored. She looked forward to speaking with him.

Tonight, she'd bring up the topic of God and see what he said. Believing as she did that God had given her a green light in his direction, it would stun her if he told her he wasn't a Christian. But she had to ask. She wanted to know what his faith was like, his background, if he went to church, and if so, where. She dreamed about him sitting beside her at church, his hand resting on hers in the pew, sharing a hymnal as they sang together. She'd smile over at him when a particularly good Bible verse was read, or when a powerful point was made in the sermon, and then they'd discuss it over coffee or lunch afterward.

She flicked away some bubbles with her finger. She'd better be careful, forming such strong feelings for a man she'd only seen twice. Oh well, third time's the charm, she thought with a laugh. Tonight was their third date, and it was time to ask him some personal questions about his past and his faith and see how they aligned with hers.

She closed her eyes. "Lord," she prayed inside her head, "let him be the one. I know, Your will be done, not mine. But please ... let him be the one for me." She opened her eyes and smiled.

A few hours later, it was almost show time. She looked down at her clothes – flat shoes, jeans and warm fleece pulled over her colorful shirt. She had no idea what Winston had planned but he'd suggested casual attire. She kind of liked the fact that he hadn't told her to dress up to go somewhere fancy. Although she enjoyed dress up dates as much as the next girl, Winston didn't really strike her as a fancy guy. Casual could be good, too.

More long-lasting. More genuine.

Her doorbell rang. She checked the time – he was very punctual. Another plus. She couldn't stand waiting for people who were late. It was something she'd had to pray about because she tended to get way too angry than the situation warranted, and she wanted God's help in fixing that. But tonight, Winston had won an extra point on the Dating Scorecard for promptness.

She swung the door open and greeted him with a big smile. "Hi! So good to see you." His beard was freshly trimmed, hair clean and fragrant. His jeans were comfortably worn and his athletic wind shirt was nicely form-fitting. "You look nice," she offered. She could tell her compliment pleased him by the easy smile it elicited on his face.

He took a step into the apartment. "You look beautiful, Tina," he said, and her heart swelled. Compliments were important in a relationship. Well, as long as they were heartfelt. And this one seemed to be. He tore his eyes from hers and looked around. "You've got a great place here," he said, glancing around the main room.

"Thanks. I've been here a couple years now. The rent is reasonable, and it serves my needs."

"You've got it decorated real cozy. I like it. In fact, I could use some tips with my place. An interior designer, I'm definitely not."

"You just need a woman's touch maybe." The words were out of her mouth and she immediately regretted them. Who was she to presume that he hadn't had a woman to help him? Or, for that matter, that she was the one to help him now?

But it didn't appear that she'd stuck her foot in her mouth because he agreed. "Definitely. It says 'bachelor pad' all the way."

She gave him a quick tour of the small place, and they ended back in the living room. "Ready to go?"

He checked his wristwatch. "Yeah, we better get going."

"Ah, do we have reservations somewhere?"

"Yes, we do. I thought we'd start the evening out with some beauty."

"There's plenty of that around here. Can't wait!"

He followed her out the door.

• • • •

WINSTON DROVE OVER to the MarshWalk located on the shoreline in Murrells Inlet. A mile-long stretch of restaurants, one after another of top-notch seafood choices. A wooden boardwalk allowed easy strolling and admiring of the phenomenal view.

The salt marsh was home to a wide variety of fish and birds, and it was the gateway to the Atlantic Ocean a little ways offshore, its location making it a favorite of many fishermen and boaters. Although a tourists' favorite, the MarshWalk was also attractive to locals like him. The boardwalk, at one point, veered out a good half mile, leaving the restaurants and shoreline behind so walkers could enjoy a stroll over the water.

FINDING LOVE FOR THE LONER

For his first official non-doggie date with Tina, he'd made reservations on the Sunset Cruise. It was about an hour in length, scheduled so they could savor the setting of the sun over the ocean. They would return and eat dinner at one of the restaurants there.

"Do you like the MarshWalk?" he asked her during the drive over.

"I do. I've only been there once, but it was pretty cool."

"It's completely different this time of year. The tourists aren't here in January so it's like a special place, a reward for the locals who are lucky enough to live here."

She turned in her seat to look at him. "Yeah, I came here in the summer and it was jammed."

He nodded. "It's fun in the summer, but I like to come when it's less crowded."

"You really love living here, don't you?"

"Oh, yeah."

"Did you grow up here?"

He maneuvered the car into the parking lot. "Yep. My parents settled here after they got married. They had me, and I never saw a reason to leave. How about you? Where did you grow up?"

"Atlanta."

"Big city. Must be very different for you here."

"Yeah, but it's a welcome change. Much slower, friendlier. People actually stop and talk to each other. I can't imagine living anywhere else now."

He nodded. "I went to a larger town for college. It was good to experience life somewhere else. But I'm back and happy to be here."

They got out of the car and he led her to the boardwalk. Her foot bumped into a parking strip and she stumbled. He reached out and grabbed her, helping her get her footing back. She looked up at him. "Thank you."

Her gaze almost took his breath away. Her eyes so expressive, her face so happy and positive. How on earth had he found himself here with her? His luck was definitely on the rise. He turned and led her to the boards but kept hold of her hand.

"I'm not usually so klutzy," she was saying, but he tried to stifle a smile. Her klutziness had given him a great excuse to hold her hand, so he was thankful.

"Which restaurant are we going to?" she asked.

He walked past several of them. "Actually, we're not going to any of them. Yet. Are you starving?"

She shrugged. "No, not really. It's fairly early."

"I had something else in mind first, then we'll do dinner." He came to a stop in a short line of people standing on the boardwalk. He pointed to a sign.

"Sunset Cruise!" she read with great gusto. "Great idea!"

He smiled appreciatively. He'd hit it out of the park, evidently, but let's face it, Tina seemed easy to please. His sandwich idea at the dog park had been met with a gusto of gratitude. Sure, the sunset cruise was a good idea, but they were offered every evening here at the MarshWalk. Her excitement over his simple plans made him wonder what she had to compare to. Had previous dates been lackluster?

How could any guy pass up on the opportunity to make her happy and see that beautiful smile?

She wrapped her arms around him and pulled him into a hug. "This'll be so fun," she said into his shoulder. He took the chance to rest his face in her hair and breathe in her fruity scent.

The boarding began and when they reached the front of the line, he gave his name. The captain's mate checked it on a list, and they boarded the boat. It was a two-level and at Tina's suggestion, they climbed the ladder to the upper floor. "Unobstructed view up here," she exclaimed, and his heart melted. She was excited as a little kid and as beautiful as the woman of his dreams. He said a silent word of gratitude to God for putting him right here in this moment.

The boat took off, through the marsh, passing by the shoreline containing beachfront homes in the South Strand until they crossed over into the open Atlantic. The waves were stronger now and at one pitch of the boat, Tina grabbed his hand. He slipped an arm behind her and pulled her close.

The sun was making its daily descent, darkness following in its wake. The ship captain brought the boat to a halt and positioned it to face the west. Muffled voices from people on the boat's first level rose to their ears. The air was just brisk enough tonight to cause a tiny puff of steam when they breathed. Tina leaned into him, resting her head on his shoulder.

"We should get a good sunset tonight. It's been so clear lately," he murmured. He didn't want to ruin the anticipation of the moment by speaking loudly. She answered in a similar low voice, "I can't wait to see it."

The colors creeped in gradually. An amazing show of artwork that happened every night if you were in the right spot at the right time. But for him and Tina, this was their first time to witness it together.

Tina pointed. "Look at the orange. It's gorgeous."

He nodded. The sun descended further and every few moments, the sky changed. They watched the progression in each other's arms, his heart filled with gratitude. Soon, other colors blended in, yellow and cream, along with the orange. The sky's dark sapphire painted a deep contrast to the shoreline's vivid lighter colors. The clouds added artistic brushstrokes.

"It's like a painting. Unbelievable," Tina said in awe.

He squeezed her shoulder while gazing up at the sky. "Thank you, God."

"Yes," she whispered. "Thank you, God."

Within a few minutes, the show was over, and the sky was dark. It was hard to believe that such astounding color only lasted five minutes, and then it was dark, and also that this was the natural part of creation and it happened night after night.

The magical spell was broken and voices grew louder. The ship's mate climbed up the stairs with a tray of plastic cups filled with a fruity liquid. "Rum punch?" she asked.

Tina said, "I'll just take the punch, no rum."

Winston nodded. "Same for me."

The woman left their drinks and climbed back down the ladder. Tina presented her beaming smile, the one he'd come to anticipate as often as possible and lifted her cup. "Cheers."

He tapped his plastic against hers and they drank. The fruity blend tasted good.

"Thank you, Winston. I'm still amazed at what we saw. I mean, I've seen sunsets before. But nothing compares to this."

Her words made him happy. He'd wanted that with her. He'd wanted a memorable shared experience, so that whenever she thought of the best sunset for the rest of her life, she'd think of him.

Mission accomplished.

They chatted easily and drank their punch as the boat made its way through the dark waters. Soon they docked at the boardwalk and everyone filed out. To stretch their legs, they walked the entire length of the MarshWalk before deciding where they would dine.

Settled into their seats beside the plate glass window overlooking the water, Winston studied his menu. Any of the fresh fish selections would be fine. They were all good and he wasn't picky. Maybe he'd just let her order first, and double whatever she selected.

The waitress stopped by their table for their drink order. He glanced at Tina. "Would you care to share a bottle of wine?" he suggested.

He was disheartened to see her frown. "No, thank you. I think I'd just like water with lemon, please."

He nodded at the waitress. "Me, too." She stepped away and he looked back at her. "I'm sorry. You're not a wine drinker?"

"No. Wine, beer, mixed drinks, none of it."

"Oh. Thanks for telling me."

She reached over the table and patted his arm. "It doesn't mean you can't drink. I mean, it doesn't bother me if you do."

He shook his head. "No, I don't drink much either. Occasionally a beer when I'm out with a group of friends. But I don't care one way or the other."

"Oh, good," she said, and sounded relieved.

"I only suggested splitting a bottle of wine to impress you with my worldliness. To be honest, I've never ordered a bottle of wine at a restaurant before. A glass occasionally."

She squeezed her lips together, a grim expression. "You don't have to impress me with your worldliness, Winston. I'm more impressed with down-to-earth."

"Good to know." He was nothing if not down-to-earth. He wouldn't have to try too hard to achieve that. He glanced back at his menu, but his mind was whirring over the exchange. There was more to the story and he couldn't help wondering about it. He set the menu aside and looked up at her. "Tina, tell me if it's none of my business. But, are you a recovering alcoholic?"

"No." She looked up and met his gaze. "And of course, it's your business. I want us to get to know each other. That includes talking about private matters."

He nodded, wondering what private matters she'd want him to fess up about.

"I'm not an alcoholic, but I have a good reason to be a teetotaler." She put her menu down as well. "I discovered alcohol in college and before I knew it, I lost all self-control. My priorities were way off. My performance in class went downhill and all I cared about was the next party."

"You shouldn't be so hard on yourself. You certainly weren't the only freshman college student to go a little crazy with a taste of independence."

She shook her head so vigorously he feared she'd pull something. "No. Not me. I entered college with my head on straight. At least I thought I did. I was a good student, a churchgoer, a good girl. I thought I knew what I wanted. But I started down the wrong road when I got to college, and a year later, I'd almost destroyed my life. I had to pull myself back and evaluate the mess I'd made. And then, make a plan for how to recover. I didn't want to live like that."

"What was in your plan?"

She heaved a deep breath and let it out. "New friends. Focus on studies. No alcohol, no parties. I had to pretty much go cold turkey."

"Extreme."

"Yeah. But when I sat back and looked at what I'd done, with a clear head, I scared myself. Here I was, a girl with so much promise in high school. My teachers wanted so much for me. My parents were so proud of me. God had always been a constant in my life. But when I truly had the chance to be independent and live my own life ... I made all the wrong choices. I did it all wrong."

He reached over and covered her hand. "But you're on the right track now."

"Yes. Never again to go off-track." Tears popped into her eyes and he reached for his cloth napkin, handed it to her. "Thanks. You must think I'm a nutcase." She dabbed her eyes.

"No, of course I don't." And he didn't. She was a woman who knew what she wanted and wasn't afraid to admit mistakes. One with a lot of emotions.

"You need to know what you're getting with me. I'm not a party girl. I don't drink. I'm not big on dancing at bars. I don't like men trying to pick me up. But I like to laugh and have a good time."

He sat still, taken aback by her direct words. "None of this surprises me."

"You're not disappointed?" she asked, and her expression was so raw he wanted to pull her into his arms to comfort her.

Disappointed? *Are you kidding me*, he wanted to say. *You're the most amazing woman I've met in a long, long time, and I feel lucky to be sitting here with you.* But he couldn't say that. Didn't have the guts, and he had no idea how she would take it. Instead, he said, "Of course not."

She looked at him a long time, and Winston tried to read her expression. She seemed relieved. Or grateful. Or both.

They were interrupted when the waitress returned with their water and asked to take their dinner order. Tina ordered shrimp with grits and he took the same thing. More silence resumed and Winston felt a need to bring the previous topic to a close.

"You seem like a person who knows what you want out of life. What you expect of yourself. And you're not afraid to go after it."

Her eyebrows went up into her bangs. "I would agree with that. Now. Are those good things or bad? In your opinion?"

"They're good."

She let out a breath followed by a chuckle. "My friends would tell you I'm Type A. A little bossy and probably less patient than I should be. There. I saved you the trouble of finding that stuff out for yourself."

He smiled at her. "You really put yourself out there. It seems like I should fess up now."

"Go for it. Only what you're comfortable with though."

He sat for a moment, thinking. "I'm not Type A. Nowhere near. My mom tells me I'm a slob, but I didn't really believe her until recently. I think I just have a different standard for what's livable than she does."

"But recently?" Tina asked.

He smiled. His bravery amped up a bit given her unabashed honesty. "I took an unbiased look around my place and realized that I'd never let *you* set foot in there before spending the whole day cleaning it."

She laughed and reached out her hand to deliver a high five. "See? Confession is good for the soul."

"Well, it's different, at any rate." He'd never admitted his sloppiness to anyone. Other than his parents, no one had ever visited his house. And when his mother went on and on about how messy it was, he had to argue with her. On behalf of bachelors everywhere. "I work all day, spend quite a bit of time with Rebel and I have several hobbies. In those remaining minutes when I'm not sleeping, cleaning my house is a low priority for me."

She shrugged. "You could hire a housekeeper."

"I could."

Then she examined him carefully. "You're not talking hoarding behavior here, are you?"

"No! Just ... messy. It's something I need to work on. And I will."

She gave him a fond smile. "I'd be happy to help you if you want."

He shook his head. "No way would I ask you to clean my house." He wanted to see how long this relationship could last, not chase her away early on.

The waitress arrived with their meals. They dug in, conversation slowing as they ate.

Later, he drove her north on Ocean Boulevard to Garden City. He parked in a public lot that allowed access to the beach. The temperature was just chilly enough, now that the sun had gone down, that they left their shoes on to walk the beach. They had discussed his favorite stories from college, then hers. Favorite subjects, best books they'd read, and movies they loved. She amazed him with her vast inventory of conversational topics. Whenever they had worn out one topic, she brought up another. He couldn't remember a night when he'd talked and shared so much.

As they walked on the dark beach, lit by the moon on the right and the high-rise buildings on their left, he slipped his hand in hers and enjoyed the simple miracle of being here with her. She turned her head and smiled at him, leaning her shoulder against him as they made their way slowly through the sand. The waves crashed and rolled, the sound lulling him into a quiet satisfaction.

"Winston?"

"Yes."

"You said something earlier that I wanted to ask you about."

He almost laughed out loud. She, of the endless conversation. "Okay?"

"When we were watching the sunset, you said, 'Thank you God.'" She looked up at him. He nodded. "Are you a Christian?"

By now her direct nature didn't surprise him. "Yeah. I am."

She squeezed his hand. "So am I. Where do you go to church?"

He hesitated. He suspected his truthful answer would not pass muster with her. She'd revealed herself tonight to be very definite in her opinions and expectations. But here he went. "I grew up going to Oceanview Church."

"Is that the one on the marsh with the beautiful big cross you can see from the ocean?"

"Yep, that's the one. Behind the altar is a plate glass window that looks out at the water."

"Hence the name," she said jokingly.

He chuckled. "Sure made it difficult to concentrate when I was a kid. Instead of listening to the pastor speak, I spent most of church service staring out that big window, wishing I was out there."

She smiled. "What about now?"

He let out a breath. "I haven't been going, other than Christmas Eve and Easter."

"Oh no!" she exclaimed. "You're not one of *those* Christians, are you? Holiday Christians?"

He hung his head, exaggerating his embarrassment. "I suppose I have become a holiday Christian."

She wrapped her palm around his forearm. "Have you and God had it out over something?"

He shook his head slowly. "Nope. Just, again, limited time due to work, et cetera."

She gave him a dubious expression. "Do you work on Sunday mornings?"

Well, she had him there. He didn't say work conflicted with the time he was in church. But after working all week, he enjoyed sleeping in on weekends. If Rebel would allow it. He deserved that after working so hard, didn't he? "No."

"Maybe you just need someone to go with. Someone to sit with. Discuss with afterwards over breakfast out."

Somehow, the thought of that special someone being Tina, didn't sound so bad. Possibly even better than sleeping in. He let out a smile. "You know, maybe you're right."

Chapter Twelve: The Matchmakers Touch Base

ROSE SHUFFLED OVER to an empty table in the coffee shop, concentrating on not spilling her hot beverage on her hand. She slid it onto the table, then turned to grab a few paper napkins. She sat, glancing over at the line of people. She tried to meet eyes with Dahlia or Lily and convince them to buy pastries for the table. She'd completely forgotten to do it herself, so focused on the topic of their meeting today: her matchmaking efforts for Winston, Lily's son.

Oh darn, here came Lily with her coffee. She set her cup down smoothly and slid into her chair. The woman moved so effortlessly, Rose thought, unlike herself, clumsy as all get out. "Were you a dancer?" she asked Lily who looked up at her in surprise.

"What?"

"You just move so gracefully, sweetie. I thought you must have a dance background."

Lily patted her hand. "Well, aren't you sweet? Um, I took tap when I was little, but I never excelled at it. My mom let me quit before I reached ballet, much to my relief."

Dahlia approached the table with a frozen fruit smoothie.

"Would anyone care for a scone or a muffin?" asked Rose brightly. She could treat, and she'd even stand in line. What a bargain for her friends.

Unfortunately, they both declined. Rose sighed. If she faced facts, she knew she didn't need the extra calories anyway. It was her wretched sweet tooth, rearing its ugly head. Too much eating over the holidays made her appetite ravenous in January. She'd just have to grab hold of her self-control and wrangle it into shape.

Besides, they had more important items to discuss.

"So ladies, I orchestrated a successful first meet between Lily's son Winston and a lovely young woman who shares his interest in dogs." She went on to describe the intentionally botched get together. She knew the two of them had stayed despite no one else showing up because she had done surveillance on them. She'd sat in her car down the block and had a view of the two of them sitting on the picnic table, getting to know each other. She didn't stay more than twenty minutes, but the fact that they were chatting and laughing seemed like a win to her.

The other matchmakers nodded and smiled. "What I don't know is, have they seen each other since then?" She turned to Lily, who shrugged.

"I have no idea." She clamped her lips. "Winston hasn't said a word to me."

Dahlia said, "Which wouldn't be a surprise to me. My son Micah doesn't confide in me about his dating life, either."

Rose nodded. "Let's brainstorm. How can we find out whether Winston liked Tina? Whether he's thinking about her. Or, maybe if he's asked her out on a date?"

Lily tapped her chin. "I could invite him over for dinner. But short of asking him, *how's your love life,* I can't really see him volunteering the information."

They all nodded. Dahlia said, "Could you ask the young lady?"

Rose's eyes went wide. "Yes! I could fake an illness for poor Scamper and see Tina at the vet's office. I could apologize for the demise of the dog park event and hope that she volunteers some information about the nice young man she met there that night. If she doesn't open up right away, I could subtly prod a little bit."

Lily smiled. "You work your magic and let us know what you find out."

• • • •

LATER THAT AFTERNOON, Rose loaded Scamper in the car with a huff. She had run into a roadblock with her quest to see Tina the Vet Tech again. She couldn't make up an imaginary illness out of the blue. First of all, the vet would charge sixty dollars for an examination. Second, Scamper was healthy.

Besides, it wasn't the veterinarian she wanted to see. It was the vet tech. One particular vet tech.

After pondering the problem for over an hour, she decided to pray about it and leave it in God's hands. She'd show up and hope that her path crossed with Tina's. *So be it, God.*

She drove the short distance to the vet's office and led Scamper in through the front door. His nose led him over to the dog food display, pulling her along behind. "Scamper, heel," she said ineffectually. Food smells trumped obeying commands, hands down. He had his nose down, following where the smells led him. Which, at the moment, was around the corner of the row of shelves to explore more selections.

Two women's voices came to her ears before she turned the corner and saw them studying the bags of dog food on the shelves.

"He's so lethargic," a woman said, "and he rarely wants to play catch anymore."

A woman in a white lab coat holding a clipboard full of papers glanced down, flipped one. "Oh, yes, he's at least ten pounds overweight. This one ...," she pulled a bag off the shelf, "would be a good choice for him."

Rose's eyes popped open. A partial plan had popped into her mind. She could ask for advice about the proper food for Scamper. The only issue was, she only wanted to ask one particular person. What best way to get face to face with Tina so she could put her plan into action?

Rose turned and pulled Scamper away from the food display. She sat down in the waiting room, where she had a direct view of the door that led to the lab. She felt quite sure that if and when Tina left the lab to visit the waiting room, it would be through that door.

Rose convinced Scamper to lie down and she took up surveillance. A thousand problems entered her mind:

What if Tina was off work today?

What if she was working, but tied up in the lab all day?

What if she came out to the waiting room but didn't have time to talk to her?

What if another tech approached her before Tina did?

She doubled down on her prayer to God, asking Him for help in getting through the barriers. He had certainly solved much bigger problems than this for her before. She had to have faith that He would come through for her now.

Minutes passed, then a half hour. She glanced at her watch and kept praying. When it was going on forty-five minutes, she started to lose hope. She'd need to go home and fix dinner, maybe come back some other time.

But then, it happened. Tina came out through the door. She could've been moving in slow motion, or maybe that was Rose's overly active imagination. But regardless, here she came, out into the waiting room. The moment Rose had been waiting for.

Far be it from her to miss her opportunity. Rose got to her feet and moved toward the shelves, pretending to peruse the food brands while keeping an eye on Tina's movement. "Excuse me," she said, pulling her pretend attention away from the shelves to notice the vet tech. "I have a question about the food. Can you help me?"

"Sure can," Tina said with a helpful smile, moving beside Rose.

"Oh, hi," Rose said, pretending to recognize her for the first time. "You've helped Scamper before. You trimmed his nails a couple weeks ago."

"I remember Scamper!" Tina said with recognition. She knelt down beside him and ruffled his ears. "Hi buddy. How are you feeling?"

"I'm so glad you're here to ask my questions to because I trust you."

"Oh, we have a great staff here. Any of us could give you advice, but I'm happy to help you. What are the symptoms you're seeing in him?"

Rose rattled off a list of symptoms that she'd previously thought of. Things that weren't true but were minor in nature and wouldn't raise concern from the medical staff. When Tina pointed to her top pick, Rose picked it up and slid it under her arm. "Great, thanks. I'm sure this'll help." She let a brief wait pass and then she said, "Hey, I'm glad we ran into each other. I wanted to follow up with you about the Lions Club outing I talked to you about last time."

Tina looked at her closely, then her eyes popped wide. "Oh yeah! Did you ever hear what happened that night?"

"What do you mean?"

"There must've been a mix-up. I attended based on the flyer that was delivered to the office, but no one showed up. It was evidently cancelled, and I didn't receive notice."

"No one? No one showed up except you?" Rose tested her acting skills, sounding amazed.

"Well, not quite no one. One other dog owner came too. He had a yellow lab. So, fortunately, our dogs got along together, and we ended up staying. But do you know if there will be a reschedule?"

Rose put a hand over her mouth in surprise. "I will definitely look into it, dear. I'm so sorry to have wasted your evening."

Tina's face softened into a happy closed-mouth grin. "Oh, it wasn't a waste, believe me."

Rose waited but Tina wasn't explaining. A prod was in order. "Oh? Why's that?"

Now Tina's smile got bigger, her white teeth showing. "The guy with the yellow lab? He and I are dating now. So no, it definitely wasn't a waste."

Rose patted her shoulder. "Oh, I'm happy for you. You never know when true love will come knocking on your door."

Tina nodded. "Well, it's too early to know if it's true love, but we've seen each other a few times, talked about everything under the sun, and he sure seems like a nice guy. Let's just say, he's a winner."

Happy tears threatened Rose's eyes. She was good at this matchmaker gig. Lily would be ecstatic when she called to fill her in.

Chapter Thirteen: It's A Numbers Game

Matchmaking Moms of Oceanview Church

WINSTON DROVE HOME from work and circled through a drive-thru line for dinner. He disliked getting into the fast food habit, but some nights it was the most logical answer. Like tonight, for example. He'd stayed late at work by thirty minutes, stuck on a phone call with a vendor. When he arrived home, he'd have to hustle through Rebel's walk, eat, and get on a phone call with LeiaPower before the evening's games started. Hamburger and fries beside him on the seat, he headed home.

Pushing through Rebel's overly enthusiastic greeting, he maneuvered her into her harness and out the door. Back inside after two miles, she plopped on the couch and rested her head on her paws, long tongue panting. Within five minutes, his phone rang. The name LeiaPower was emblazoned across his screen. His pulse increased as he answered, "Hi, Leia."

"Hi, Winston." Her sultry voice caused a shudder in his breath. "How are things going for you tonight?"

"Great. How about you?"

A giggle tinkled over the line. "Better now that I get to speak to you."

He shook his head, his brain whirring in confusion. He should be thrilled that she was so complimentary of him. Her

FINDING LOVE FOR THE LONER

praise was an ego rush, no doubt. But it made him uncomfortable, unleashing in him an impulse to fight it. Was it because of his budding relationship with Tina? Or was it because her adoration of him was wrong in God's eyes?

All he knew was, he was totally out of his league and had no idea how to handle it.

He cleared his throat. "So, you wanted to share with me your plans for the workshop proposal?"

"That's right. I thought I'd start with a bang and share all your impressive credentials. Really knock 'em dead and let them know who they're dealing with here. You know, top Star Battler champion four years running. Highest scoring fighter pilot, most clean kills career-level, winningest team captain two years in a row."

She rattled off his accomplishments in the gaming world and he soon found it hard to listen. A buzzing in his ears made him feel detached. He forced himself to focus on what she was telling him. Yes, some could say he was a leader in the Star Battler online game. But this was not an achievement that caused him a great deal of pride. There was nothing wrong with it particularly, but it definitely wasn't something he openly talked about with his friends, with his parents, with anyone.

When you broke it down, what did all those accomplishments mean? It meant he'd spent an inordinate number of hours every night, sitting here alone on his couch, playing a game. He had an aptitude for it, and he'd gotten good at it.

So what?

What could he have done with all those hundreds, no, thousands of hours? What would God have had him do with all those hours instead of playing games, if only he'd been tuned into God's will?

For that matter, how long had it been since he'd actually been tuned into God at all?

"Then I'll turn it over to you, applause, applause, applause, and I'd like you to pick two or three of your classic moves to demonstrate. You give some thought to which ones, offensive or defensive. I don't have to include the exact moves in the proposal, just that you'll demo some advanced plays. Then you'll turn it over to me, and I'll start discussing why I sought you out as a mentor, how I winded up on your team, and what I've learned from you."

He let out a choke, unintentionally.

"Winston? Are you okay?" she asked, her voice concerned.

"Yes, sorry. It's just, Leia, I gotta tell you ..."

"What?" Her voice was flat, like she was expecting the worst.

"I, uh ... I don't know. It just sounds so ...boastful. Self-centered. Like I think the world revolves around me."

She sniffed and paused. "Well. First of all, I'm the one presenting it, not you. I think you're wrong. I don't think it'll come off like you're self-centered. I think it'll come off like I look up to you for your Star Battler skills. And it's true, I do." Her voice softened. "And I think our particular world does revolve around you, Winston. You are the best player in Star Battler history. But for some reason, you don't seem to realize that."

He shrugged, even though he was alone, and no one could see him. "But Leia, Star Battler is a relatively new game. How long's it been around?"

"Four years."

Well, there you go, he thought. He was going to guess five, max. He let a moment of silence pass while he thought this through. Crushing Leia's dreams of being a workshop leader at GamingCon would make him feel horrible. If he could help her achieve her dreams, he'd naturally want to do it. But the boastful nature of the workshop made him cringe. Regardless of whether she thought he was a big deal he knew he wasn't. And he didn't want to stand on a false pedestal in a room full of adoring gamers and make them think that he agreed with what Leia was saying.

"Leia," he said, thinking of a possible angle. "Tell me more about GamingCon. What types of games are represented there?"

"Oh, all of them," she replied. She went on to name a half dozen popular online games, including some much longer-term games than theirs.

"How many workshops are offered?"

"Oh gosh, I don't know. Maybe a dozen? Fifteen?"

"And how many attendees are there usually?"

"Let me Google how many attended last year." A tapping sound came over the line. "Ten thousand. Wow."

Winston went back to ruminating. Ten thousand attendees and only fifteen workshops. How many workshop proposals would be submitted for the judging panel to whittle down to fifteen? And how impressive would the workshops need to be to float to the top? It had to be a highly competitive exercise.

And if all Leia's workshop had to offer was his Star Battler credentials and a demo, what's the chance that it would be selected?

He had to think the chances were close to nil.

So, he could approve Leia's submission of the workshop to the committee, knowing it had very little chance of being approved. He didn't have to be the bad guy and disappoint Leia, and he'd get out of this ridiculous commitment.

Problem solved.

"Leia, go ahead."

A gasp of happiness. "Really? Seriously?"

"Yeah. What the heck, right? You only live once." Easy being philosophical when he knew she stood very little chance of being approved.

"You are the absolute best," she gushed. "I'm serious. This means so much to me. You'll need to let me take you out to dinner when we're in Myrtle Beach."

"Myrtle Beach? You're coming to Myrtle Beach?"

"Yeah, silly. GamingCon this year is at Myrtle Beach. Didn't you know?"

His throat went dry. "No, I didn't." He knew he was about to cross a major line in the online ethical rules, but he had to know. "Leia, where do you live?"

She hesitated, since she knew the online protocol as well as he did. She decided to breach them as well, because she answered in a hushed tone, "St. Louis."

She'd have to fly in. He, however, was twenty minutes away from the conference. He couldn't decide if that made him feel better or worse. Regardless, it was almost time to join the game. "Keep me posted on the judging decision."

"I sure will. And thanks again. I mean it. I couldn't do this without you."

• • • •

FINDING LOVE FOR THE LONER

TINA STOOD IN FRONT of her stove, using a wooden spoon to stir and stir and stir. Her pot of hearty vegetable beef soup was simmering, the aroma making her stomach growl with anticipation. She didn't do a great deal of cooking, but this was one of those no-lose recipes she'd made many, many times and it always turned out delicious. It was, however, a big time commitment. Between browning the chuck roast, chopping the meat and all the vegetables, boiling it, then slow simmering for almost three hours, it was an effort. But every time she ate it, she knew it was worth it.

She laid the spoon down and checked the cornbread muffins in the oven. They looked good. Maybe just a few more minutes. Checking the time, she saw with satisfaction that everything would be ready just in time for Winston's arrival.

She leaned against the counter, keeping an eye on the pot to make sure it didn't over boil. Glancing over at the table, she gave a half smile at how she'd set it, two place settings with a bowl and a small plate. She moved to the refrigerator and checked for the fifth time – she was fully stocked on drinks. She could offer him iced tea, lemonade or iced water with a slice of lime. An Old-Fashioned Dump Cake, one of her mother's favorite recipes from her childhood, sat cooling on the counter.

Yes, she was nervous. Yes, she was jittery. But who wouldn't be? This was the first time she'd ever invited a guy she was interested in over for dinner at her place. A completely home-cooked dinner in a place she called home. Being the perfectionist she was, this evening offered room for failure, and the way to avoid failure was to plan and plan and plan some more. Every moment of the meal had been pondered and executed, from menu selection, grocery shopping and cooking. The apartment was immaculate, due to her massive cleaning spell starting last night, and continuing all day today. The place virtually sparkled, and she could smell the cleanness in the air.

All she needed now was to welcome him in, serve him and eat. She could do it.

She peeked at the cornbread again, deciding they were browned enough to come out. Tugging on her oven mitt, she pulled them out and set the kitchen timer to let them cool.

Her hand shook a little and her chest reflected a tiny bit of anxiety, but she was used to this part of her personality. Honestly, she'd lived with it her entire life. She casually referred to herself as a Type A personality, but if there was an A+++, she'd qualify. *You're a worrywart,* her mother always told her. *You're hyperactive,* her roommates in college had said. *Relax,* probably a million people had told her throughout her life.

But she couldn't, and she'd long ago admitted to herself that this was her. Which had always made it difficult to carry on long-term relationships, either platonic or romantic. Okay, she was difficult, she recognized. But she meant well. She tried to mask her anxious ways. She just wasn't always successful.

The timer dinged and she carefully popped the cornbread out of the muffin tin, pulled over the breadbasket she'd already lined with a towel, and arranged them in. Her mother told her that opposites attract, and in her case, her best chance at finding a forever type of guy would be to find a calm, easygoing guy. Finding another high-energy domineering type would be a recipe for disaster. She didn't know if that was necessarily true, but the few boyfriends she'd had with a similar personality as hers, she had to admit she was ready to strangle them after a half dozen dates, and them her.

When she thought about Winston, her racing heart calmed. There was something about him that made her relax a little. He was steady and easygoing. The fact that he was good-looking and nice and polite were icing on the cake.

She'd invited him over for dinner for a couple reasons. Number one, to see him in her own setting. Would he fit in here? Or, would he clash like a bull in a china shop? Would they be able to enjoy themselves during a simple evening at home, or would they need the entertainment of an evening out to get along?

And number two, would he appreciate her dinner-making efforts? Would her cooking skills please him? Would he be quick with the compliment, or hard to satisfy?

Her doorbell rang. She checked the oven clock. He was right on time. Another point for Winston, before the date even began. She turned off the burner under the soup and went to the door.

She swung it open, and the sight of him overwhelmed her senses. His sweet face that she'd gotten accustomed to seeing, his wavy hair that gave her the urge to touch. His scent reached her nostrils and she couldn't help breathing it in. Motionless, she let it all flood over her, then she grounded herself by staring into his beautiful blue eyes, the color of the ocean.

"Hi," she said, not surprised that she sounded breathless. What a greeting. And he hadn't even said a word.

"Hi there," he said softly with a smile that started small and grew.

"I'm sorry for staring," she said, reached for his hands and pulled him in.

"No problem at all. Gave me a chance to stare at you, too. You look beautiful, Tina." He stepped into the living room and looked around. "I like it in here. Really nice."

Tina gave her living room a look through fresh eyes. She'd furnished the room in the blues and aqua greens of the sea, with sandy-colored carpet and walls. The beach theme continued with her accent pillows, lamps and wall hangings. She'd had fun decorating her Murrells Inlet apartment with beachy stuff. It was a novelty being so close to the beach. But after a year, she was accustomed to it now and barely gave it a second look. "Thank you, Winston."

He lifted his nose and sniffed. "Something sure smells good. What is it?"

She smiled and gestured. "Come and see." She led him into the kitchen, the pot on the stove practically brimming over with beef, carrots, celery, black eyed peas, okra and a bajillion spices.

"Oh my my my," he said, leaning close to the pot and sniffing. "How did you know beef vegetable soup was one of my favorite meals? And Lordy be, cornbread?" He rubbed his stomach. "We're going to eat good tonight."

She giggled. His natural southern accent had emerged. She'd never heard it so close to the surface before. "I'm so glad you're excited about what I made." She opened the refrigerator and pointed. "There's a couple drink choices in here. I'll let you decide what you want while I take the soup and the cornbread to the table."

Soon they were eating, the steam of the hot soup joining the heavenly aroma. Winston went still after putting the first spoonful in his mouth, his eyes drifting closed. After swallowing, he said, "Oh, Tina. You're smart, ambitious, good with animals. Now I know you're an awesome cook too. This is delicious."

Tina couldn't help but grin. Being as achievement-oriented as she was, she liked getting recognition for her results. If the result was bad, it was okay to hear about it because she was always looking to improve. However, she worked so hard at everything that her results were rarely bad. And the danger of always doing stuff well is that people assumed you didn't need the praise. That you're just used to doing everything well.

It wasn't true. When she worked hard at something and did a good job, it did our heart good to hear some praise.

"Thank you, Winston." Three compliments and he'd only been here fifteen minutes. This man was going to spoil her.

They ate and chatted easily, Tina telling him about the puppy she'd treated today for consuming a grape. "She was in bad shape, vomiting and her blood pressure was way down."

Winston laid down his spoon. "For eating a grape?"

"Yep. Grapes can be toxic for dogs. It can actually be very serious. Worst case scenario, it can kill a puppy."

Winston shook his head. "I'm glad you told me. I don't think I've given Rebel grapes, but I have given her apples before and carrots."

"Those are fine. But grapes and raisins, keep away from dogs."

The dinner went on. Winston consumed two big bowls of soup and three cornbread muffins. Then she remembered. "I hope you saved room for dessert."

He had just pushed his plates away and leaned back in his chair. "Dessert?"

She laughed. "No room?"

He took a big breath and let it out. "None at the present time but give me an hour and I should be okay for dessert."

"Here's an idea. Why don't we take Max for a walk? Exercise could help you digest."

"Great idea."

They took their time leaving the table. Winston offered to clear the table of dishes while Tina outfitted Max for their walk. In a few minutes, they met at the front door.

Outside, Tina chose a route. "Are you up for a couple miles?"

"Sure. I'm a healthy young man," he replied, and the corners of his mouth turned up.

"Do you ever run?" she asked, suddenly curious.

"Not unless I have to. And I rarely have to. So, no."

She laughed. "I was thinking about training for a half marathon, but I wish I had someone to train with."

His pause extended. She glanced over at him while they walked.

"I was hoping the subject would change in case that was an invitation," he said.

"You're not into it, huh?"

"Not particularly. But I wish you well in your endeavors."

She smacked his arm. "You crack me up."

They walked in comfortable quiet. Their steps took them off the sidewalk and onto the grassy berm adjacent to the parkway. She said, "I wanted to take you to a park we have up here, but the sidewalk doesn't go the whole way. Are you comfortable walking on the grass for a little ways?"

He looked up. "It's getting kind of dark."

"The park is well lit. It's only a couple of blocks that's not."

"Okay."

They continued walking, Max leaning uncharacteristically on his collar. She squinted, trying to see what was distracting him. Then she saw it: a squirrel. His perpetual enemy. Maybe she should have put his special harness on that discouraged pulling. "Max, heel! Come on boy. Stop pulling."

Winston reached out a hand. "Do you want me to take him?"

His offer triggered an involuntary response. She harbored a long-standing pet peeve about men assuming that women were damsels in distress and they needed to help the "little lady" out. Which in her case, was absolutely not true. She could handle very well indeed, thank you.

Without planning her response, she replied a sharp "no." He withdrew his hand and most likely, his offer.

She looked over at him, seeking out his expression in the growing darkness. "I'm sorry, I didn't ..." But before she could finish her apology, Max lunged and suddenly, his collar and leash were lying in the grass. And Max was on the run.

"Max!" she screamed frantically.

Winston shot off like a rocket. She hurried to keep up with him. They were running blindly, the gloominess around them not allowing clear vision. Suddenly, a tiny burst of light. Winston had pulled out his phone and activated the flashlight function. Relief seeped through her for a split second. Only for a split second. Because in the new light, she witnessed what happened next.

About forty yards ahead, Max dashed up the incline of the berm and into the street, his figure illuminated by the headlights of an oncoming car.

Sounds collided. Her own shriek, Winston's yell, Max's squeal of pain, and the screeching of brakes. She froze. Her body and her mind disengaged from each other and she was left somewhere in the void.

But not Winston. She watched dumbly as he covered the distance to the car, scooped Max up off the pavement and carried him carefully back to safety. He laid the big dog on the soft grass while the driver got out of the car.

"I didn't see him coming," the man was saying. "He came out of nowhere." The driver's voice was full of regret and Tina knew she should say something to him. She watched as he ran back to his car and turned on his hazards to prevent further collision. Then he returned to the side of the road to kneel over her beloved Max, along with Winston.

The sight of the two men tending to Max snapped her back to action. She darted over to the huddle and knelt. She cupped Max's big face with her hands and studied his eyes. "He's in shock." His pupils were dilated, he was staring. His pants were occasionally laced with a painful whine. She let her veterinary knowledge kick in. She needed to examine him to determine the extent of his injuries.

"She's a vet," she heard Winston tell the driver.

"Good. His leg is bleeding and bent a little weird," the driver commented.

Tina got to work. She quickly conducted a full-body exam, murmuring words of comfort to her Max, leaving the right back leg for last. She turned to Winston. "I think the leg is the extent of his injuries. I don't see anything anywhere else. Now, come to his head while I examine his leg."

Winston moved quickly to do as she said. With Winston comforting Max, she positioned herself at the hind leg. Sure enough, there was a fracture that would need to be set and cast, and a wound that needed to be sutured.

"He needs emergency care. Right now." She sought out Winston's gaze, and he must have known her urgency. He said, "I'll run back to the apartment and get my car."

The driver, now Tina saw was a teenager or just barely in his twenties, said, "No, let's go together in my car. It'll save time."

Tina wasn't going to argue with him. "Let's go." She slipped off her jacket and concocted a temporary sling for the leg. Winston slipped his off and laid it on the back seat. He and the driver counted, coordinating a joint lift worthy of an expert EMT team. They carried the dog and rested him on the seat, Tina climbing in behind to sit beside him. She wrapped her arms around him and kept up a steady string of words to let him know she was there for him.

Hours later, after rushing to the emergency veterinarian, watching the doctor take care of the leg, receiving care instructions, returning to the waiting room to find both Winston and the driver (who she learned was named Pete) waiting for word, they drove back to the apartment. The two men carried the sedated dog up to her front door and laid him gently onto his dog bed inside.

She stood watching her boy for a few moments, ignoring the movement behind her, until she came to her senses. She turned and Pete was on his way out the door. "Wait!"

He turned and looked at her.

"I wanted to thank you for all you did. It was so kind of you to take up your entire evening to take us to the ER vet and back home again."

He shook his head. "It was the least I could do after hitting him."

Winston turned to him. "It wasn't your fault. He got off his leash and darted. You couldn't have avoided it."

Tina couldn't have said it better herself. "I'd like to compensate you for your time. It's the least I can do."

Pete shook his head, turning down her offer. "I insist," she said.

Winston squeezed her hand. "I already did. He's good to go."

Tina stared into his eyes, emotions flying through her body at such a fast rate that she didn't know what to do next. So, she just whispered, "Thank you."

. . . .

WINSTON CLOSED THE door behind Pete and turned. Tina stretched out beside Max on the floor, curling her body around his, and wrapping her arms around him. She whispered into his ear and Max closed his eyes to rest.

"I bet he'll sleep well tonight. The meds they gave him will help with rest too."

She nodded in acknowledgement.

Winston watched the two of them. It had been a frightening moment but thank God Max had escaped with nothing but a broken leg. The doctor expected no problems in recovery. Four weeks in the cast, with Tina helping him with basic care and he'd be as good as new. Not wanting to interrupt their moment of closeness, he found himself whispering. "Can I get anything for you?"

She shook her head, giving all her attention to the patient.

Winston glanced around and located his jacket. He was pulling it on when he heard her soft voice. "Don't go. Please?"

"No, of course not. I'm here as long as you need me." He took a few steps to reach her side and folded his legs, sitting on the floor beside her. He placed a hand on her shoulder.

"Will you lay with me?"

Winston nodded and stretched out, lying on his side and spooning her form. She continued to stroke Max. They lay quietly.

"I'm sorry," she whispered. Then she turned her face in his direction. "I'm sorry, Winston."

He frowned. "For what? This wasn't your fault. It was an accident."

She let out a deep breath. "Well, I shouldn't have had him in a collar. He would've been much more secure in his harness and this never would've happened. He saw a squirrel and got excited."

He ran his hand up and down her arm. "You didn't do anything wrong. You can't second guess every decision. You didn't mean for him to get hurt, but he did. And you did everything right to get him taken care of. He's going to be fine now."

She nodded her head in front of him, up, down, up, down. She turned in his direction again. "It definitely wasn't my finest hour tonight."

"What do you mean?"

"You were witness to many of my faults tonight. I'm stubborn, I freeze up when I get scared, I sometimes assume the worst of people. I have so much work to do on myself."

Winston didn't reply because quite honestly, he was speechless. How could she be so critical of herself? She was as close to perfect as he'd ever encountered in someone. She was smart, ambitious, successful, beautiful. He was still counting his lucky stars to be here with her, in what was looking more and more like a relationship.

He was trying to decide how to respond when her shoulders started shaking. She buried her face in Max's scruff and when she pulled out for a breath, it was wet.

He squeezed his arms tighter around her. He didn't want to pull her away from Max, but he wanted her to know he was there for her. He shushed her, which he hoped was comforting. "Don't cry. You were perfect tonight. Everything turned out fine. Don't be so hard on yourself, sweetheart. Shhh, shhh."

Her sobs continued. Although he wanted to stop them, he didn't know how. Instead he held her tight, murmuring in her ear.

Chapter Fourteen: Winston's a Keeper

ON SUNDAY, AFTER THE service ended, Tina kept an eye on the departing crowd, hoping to catch sight of Becky. She was starting to give up hope, convinced her friend had skipped services today, when she finally saw her brown hair and friendly smile. She zoomed to her side and grabbed her arm.

"Oh!" Becky exclaimed. "Tina!"

"I need a friend," Tina said. Becky nodded and they headed for the coffee line. Once both cups were poured and doctored, they found a couple arm chairs in a private corner. Tina quickly filled her in on the car accident and the doctoring of Max's leg.

"You must've been so scared. I know how crazy you are about Max. I'm so glad he's going to be okay. Praise God it wasn't any worse."

"Yeah, I was terrified. In fact, in the face of the tragedy, I froze. It was weird, like I was watching a movie and I couldn't move." She drew a deep breath and let it shakily out.

"Oh, sweetie," Becky murmured. She leaned close and grabbed Tina's free hand. "You were distraught! Anyone would've frozen. It's understandable."

Tina gave her head a fierce shake. "But not Winston. He had a clear head while I was freaking out. He stepped in and filled in all my blanks. He was a hero that night. I don't know what I would've done without him."

Becky watched her, eyes opening wide. "Wow. Could it be? Am I hearing what I think I'm hearing?"

Tina looked away, a hot flush on her cheeks.

"I think you may be in love, Miss Mitchell." Becky moved her hand to Tina's forearm and squeezed it.

"No," Tina said immediately, then wondered. "Really?" She looked at Becky.

"Could be! He sure seems like a good guy. And he's devoted to you and Max, that's for sure."

"Do you think?" She searched Becky's face. She was so out of her element here. She'd never been in love. Never even close. With her history of making bad choices in the man department, she had trouble trusting her instincts. "He's got many good qualities. He's kind. He's always complimenting me, and I've never heard him say a bad word about anyone. Ever. He's easy to talk to. We could talk about any subject under the sun and I can't imagine him getting mad or upset. He's very easy going and laid back."

Her friend nodded, staring at her.

"I know what you're thinking. He's the total opposite of me." She glanced at Becky, who laughed.

"You're a good person. You're just sort of ... intense. And driven." She paused to think, rushing on at the change in Tina's expression. "But those aren't bad qualities!"

"No, of course not," she said sarcastically.

"I'm willing to bet that he likes those things about you. People aren't usually drawn to someone exactly like themselves.

A good couple fills in where the other lacks. A really good couple is better together than separate."

"You complete me," she recited from a movie she'd seen once.

Becky laughed. "Exactly."

Tina set that aside in her mind to consider in more depth later. She and Winston seemed to fill in spaces where the other lacked. But they didn't know each other fully yet. Would Winston's easygoingness annoy her as time went on? More importantly, if Winston got to know her better, would her intensity drive him crazy? The night of the accident, she'd jumped to a misinterpretation of his offer for help. She assumed he thought she was unable to take care of herself and Max, offering help because she was weak.

But now that a few days had passed, she felt sure that was not his intention at all. Why did she jump to that conclusion?

Would she drive him away if he knew all her faults?

Becky was speaking so she tuned back in. "I'd really like to meet this new man."

"Why don't I invite him to church with me? See how he likes it, and I'll introduce you and you can give me your expert opinion."

"I don't know about expert opinion, but I'll give you my honest reaction to him."

"Deal."

• • • •

THE FIRST WEEK AFTER the car accident, Max struggled to get around with one back leg in a plaster cast. According to the vet, it was okay to put his weight on it. But since he couldn't bend it, he didn't like to walk. He usually just remained stretched out on the floor. When it was time to go outside to relieve himself, Tina would have to tug him to his feet, and help him limp pitifully out the door on a leash. When Winston was there, he'd lift the heavy dog and carry him outside, then back in when he was done.

It didn't go unnoticed by her that once Winston recognized the need, he worked hard to fill it. He'd stop by in the evening, regardless of whether they had plans together, simply to take Max out. Even more impressive, he'd stop by early in the morning on his way to work to help Max relieve himself in the morning, as well.

"You don't have to," she protested. "He needs to learn to walk in the cast. He's going to be in it for a month!"

Winston waved his hand. "I don't mind. Besides, he'll learn eventually. He's adjusting to a change in life which is always difficult. Might as well try to make it easy on the poor guy." And he'd bend his knees, wrap his arms under the big dog and carry him outside with nary a complaint.

The guy really was amazing.

Fortunately, by the second week, Max had learned to hobble around without help. She'd returned home from work one evening and he'd met her at the door. It took her a moment to realize what was different that evening, from any other. Then, she sank to her knees, wrapped her arms around his neck and murmured, "Good boy! What a good boy!"

The only bad thing about Max's successful adjustment was she saw Winston less. But she reminded herself, she'd never wanted to be the damsel in distress. She'd always wanted to enter a relationship with a man on equal footing. Although Winston had been a huge help since the accident, she didn't want to slip into the pattern of needing him or expecting him to help her.

On Saturday night, she and Winston were attending a beachfront music festival featuring local bands, a new one playing every hour or so. They had gotten into the habit of alternating the date planning, and this one was Winston's idea. She was excited to be doing something out of the house and not involving Max. Of course, she loved him to death, but he was recovering nicely, to the point where he could manage being home alone one evening. And Mama needed a night out.

Winston arrived at her apartment door. She opened it and she immediately heard the thump of Max's tail against the hardwood floor. Winston leaned in to give her a quick kiss, then headed straight to her dog. He knelt to one knee and held Max's head in his hands. "Hey boy, you're looking good. How are you feeling? How's that leg?"

"He's had a good day. Seems like the pain is about gone."

Winston ruffled his fur, gave him a final pat and got to his feet. Turning back to her, he pulled her up against him. "Now for a more proper greeting." He dipped his head and laid his lips on hers, the warmth sending a shiver down her spine. The man smelled so good, looked so good, and yes, kissed well too. In the weeks they'd been seeing each other, she'd grown phenomenally fond of him.

He pulled back and smiled at her. "Ready for some outdoor music?"

"Yep. I assume I'll need a jacket?"

They had flipped the calendar to February, which was still winter in the Grand Strand, but mild compared to where she'd come from. Some days hit a low of forty degrees, but they were rare. Today the temperature had maxed out at sixty-five, although it would be chillier when the sun went down.

He helped her with her coat. Soon they were making their way on the beach in Garden City. A hotel had set up this annual festival, Tina guessed, to help with the decrease of business in the offseason. A stage had been set up on the sand, along with a dozen rows of folding chairs. Food trucks parked on the sand offered a variety of tacos, hamburgers, hot dogs and ribs. A tiki bar was set up to dispense drinks.

The bands had already begun, and the sound of 80's rock filled the air. The chairs were partially filled, and many people were dancing barefoot in the sand. She turned to him. "Do you dance?"

His eyebrows darted up. "Hmmm. Not often. But I would. If you wanted to, that is."

She shook her head. "You don't enjoy it?"

He shrugged. "Not particularly."

"True confession, I don't either."

He gave an exaggerated *whew*. He gave her an odd expression. "Then why did you ask me?"

She chuckled. "I want to learn all there is to know about you. I didn't know if you liked to dance or not. Now I know." She took his hand. "But you were willing to dance with me if I wanted to. Why?"

"Although I wouldn't choose to dance, I wouldn't deny you if you wanted to. No skin off my back, as long as you aren't embarrassed by my moves. Or lack thereof."

She watched him quietly.

"What?"

"You're just so ..."

"What?" he said suspiciously.

"Amazing. That's what I was going to say."

He shook his head. "What's so amazing?"

She started walking and he came as well. "I need to learn to be more like you. You're very sure of yourself. Of your personality. Of who you are."

He stopped walking and faced her. "You got all that from me being willing to dance with you?"

She huffed out a breath, wondering if she could put this into words for him. "I've become sort of defensive over the years. I've been so determined to be independent, to be my own person, that I've forgotten how to bend. To be flexible. To do something for someone else, even if it wasn't my choice. But you. You do that so naturally. And it's not weakness. It's just ... goodness."

He lifted a shoulder. "It's no big deal."

"It isn't to you. Because you're kind. And secure. Letting another person have their way doesn't take anything away from you. But me ... I guess I always have my guard up. Especially with a man. If I want one thing and a man wants another, there's no way I would let him win. I would feel like I let him take advantage of me." She sniffed and brushed a strand of hair out of her eye. "But it's never even occurred to you to think of it that way, has it?"

"The way I win is if you're happy. Because if you're happy, I'm happy."

She stared at him in the setting sun and she knew she was looking at the best man she'd ever dated. Possibly the best man she'd ever met. In that moment, she decided she'd try to be more like him. She was well aware of her faults, and she needed to evolve. He made her want to improve.

The idea was so unusual she didn't know quite what to make of it.

"What are you thinking now?" he asked. "I can practically see the gears churning up there." He tapped her forehead lightly and grinned.

It was a risk to tell him the truth. But she wanted to tell him. "I was just thinking that I'm going to work on my faults. I don't want to be so defensive. I want to be kinder and more considerate of others. You've inspired me." A pause passed and she tugged on his hand. "Let's go check out those food trucks. I'm hungry."

He walked for a moment and then said casually, "You know you don't need to change anything for me, right? I don't see all these faults that you're referring to. I think you're amazing just the way you are."

She closed her eyes and enjoyed a warmth flushing through her system. "And that's one of the reasons I like you so much. But I need to do this. For myself." She couldn't fully explain it. He made her want to be a better person. Not more like him ... someone who fit better with him. That's what it boiled down to.

They headed back to a carefree evening, the sounds of the ocean waves crashing in the distance, the sand under their feet, musical notes in the air and joy in her heart.

Chapter Fifteen: Be All You Can Be

VANESSA SWUNG BY WINSTON'S cubicle like she did every day. "Ready for break?"

"Yep." He finished documenting the call he'd just made, closed the record and hibernated his computer. They headed down the aisle to the break room.

Settled at the table with hot drinks, Vanessa said, "You know who I haven't heard you talk about lately? Tina."

Winston kept his eyes trained on the coffee cup, wondering if an ignore tactic would work on his persistent buddy.

"Hey." She made him jump, not only with the tone of her voice, but also a slug in his arm. "Dish."

He sighed. "Yeah. We're seeing each other. We're doing good."

"So why has she become a No-Go Zone in our conversation topics?"

Winston started to argue, and realized, Vanessa was right. He hadn't felt comfortable talking about his relationship with Tina lately. And why was that? Because it was going so well he didn't want to jinx it? Or because he'd always subscribed to the "Kiss don't tell" philosophy. Not that he'd had many opportunities to put it into action. But in theory, he agreed.

"I don't know ...," he started, and Vanessa interrupted him.

"Oh wait. I do!" She leaned across the table, pulling closer to him, a devious smile on her face. "I know what this is. You're in love with her!"

"What? No!" It was an automatic response, not wanting Vanessa to have anything with which to lord over his head. But in all honesty, he had begun wondering the same thing himself. Vanessa was married. Maybe she could advise him. He lowered his voice, looking around for potential eavesdroppers. "Actually, I could use your advice. But you have to swear not to laugh or, God forbid, repeat this conversation to anyone else."

She made a zipping motion over her lips. "I swear."

He let out a slow breath. "How do I know if this is love? How do I differentiate between love and just dumb luck that such an incredible woman is in a relationship with me?"

He knew he'd left the door open to her for ridicule, good-natured though it may be. But to her credit, she didn't go that route. She smiled at him for a moment. "Do you think about her constantly when you're not with her? Do you picture her face and replay conversations you've had? Does your heart want to explode when you see her?" She paused like she expected an answer, but he wasn't about to agree to all that Valentine's Day romance stuff. She went on, "Then, it could be love!"

"Could be? That's no more than I knew before I asked you."

"Well, it's not like you can take a test, figure your score and determine definitely that it's love. It's emotional. Why put a label on it? You love being with her. She seems to feel the same about you. Go with it and see where it goes. I mean, you're not planning on proposing marriage, are you?"

"No, I'm not." Just go with it. That seemed like good advice. If he could manage to just relax and continue to be himself, maybe this thing would turn out to be the real thing.

"Okay. Just don't blow it," she said with a laugh. But little did she know that throwaway comment was exactly what he was afraid of. Not that he'd admit it to Vanessa, but he needed to know: how did he avoid blowing it?

"Okay. So, I may be in love, I may not be, but just keep going and see how it goes."

"That's about it, tiger." She glanced at her phone and pointed at it. "We'd better make our way back."

He nodded and got up. "Tina made an interesting comment the other night. She said she wanted to work on some of her faults so that her personality goes better with mine."

Vanessa came to a halt so fast he left her in the dust a few steps before he stopped and turned with a questioning look.

"If you're looking for a concrete sign that she's in love with you, that's it."

"Really?"

She shook her head and started walking again. "Dense. So dense. Don't hesitate to run this stuff by me, Winston. You need all the help you can get."

• • • •

THAT EVENING, WINSTON returned home, opened his front door and greeted a very enthusiastic Rebel. Wrangling on her harness amidst her tail wags and jumps, they took their nightly walk. Back home, he fed her and finally they settled into the couch and relaxed.

Throughout the walk, his mind ran over Tina's desire to improve on her faults. Well, shouldn't he be considering his own faults and deciding what he could improve on too? He didn't have to search far before he came up with his first fault: his lack of housekeeping skills. Being in a relationship inevitably meant inviting Tina over to his house. And he couldn't allow her in here without doing some serious scrubbing.

Well, there was no time like the present.

He changed into comfortable clothes and got busy. It was a small house, but there were at least six rooms that needed intense attention. He gathered his supplies: bucket, soapy water, sponges, scrub brushes, broom, mop, cleaning detergents. And he dove in.

He didn't come up for air until it was all done. He had cleaned both floors of his house until the hard wood gleamed, the baseboards were scrubbed, the bathroom sparkled, and the kitchen would've appealed to a celebrity chef. Clothes were folded and put away in the bedroom, beds were made. He checked the time. It had taken him four hours. Wow. Enough of a time commitment that he never wanted to let it get out of hand again.

If he picked up after himself each and every day, it would take minimal effort to keep it presentable. And if he spent an hour a week scrubbing the kitchen and bathroom and keeping the dog hair picked up ... maybe, *just maybe*, he could recover from this slob habit.

He flung himself onto the couch, panting from all the effort. He glanced around. He had to admit the place looked great. Although he'd become accustomed to the mess, he realized that it wasn't normal to live like that. He hadn't grown up in a messy house. And he was certain Tina wasn't messy. If he had a prayer of having a committed relationship with her, he didn't ever want her to see that side of him. He would beat his messy tendencies and keep his place clean. For her and for himself.

He dragged himself to his feet and headed for the kitchen, more than ready for some nourishment. When he was sitting at the table eating a sandwich, the thought came to his mind of one other person who would be absolutely thrilled to see the New and Improved Winston and his Clean House: his mom. Although it wasn't her persistent nagging that had caused him to change his ways, he'd finally gotten around to where she'd wanted him all along.

He'd invite her and Dad over to see the result. And besides, it was probably time to introduce his parents to Tina, so he could use that visit to prepare them. He smiled, thinking how thrilled his parents, Mom especially, would be to hear that he was seeing someone. They'd wanted that for him for so long.

Mid-bite, his phone buzzed, indicating a text coming in. He pulled the phone over. LeiaPower had sent him a text? He tapped it.

"*U ok? U missed the battle 2nite.*"

He stared at the message, astounded. Three nights a week, for more years than he could count, his evening routine had been the same. Spending four hours cleaning house tonight meant he was a no-show for his game.

Most surprising, he hadn't thought twice about missing Star Battler. His life was changing, and for the better.

He tapped a reply. "*I'm fine. Sorry. Hope all went well.*"

Then he powered down his phone so he wouldn't be drawn into an ongoing conversation.

Chapter Sixteen: Winston Shares Some Big News

LILY BUCKLED HER SEATBELT and looked over at James starting the car. "Wonder what this impromptu invitation is about?"

James paused, shrugged and backed up the car. "Our son can't invite the folks over for pizza spur of the moment?"

"He *can*. But does he ever?"

James chuckled. "Don't look a gift horse in the mouth, sweetheart. When's the last time you saw him?"

She frowned, calculating in her mind. It had been several weeks. Although they lived in the same area, they all had their lives. She hated to intrude on him, but she rarely went more than a couple weeks without reaching out. "True. I'm thrilled that he invited us, regardless of whether it was sudden or not."

"You're so suspicious."

"Do you think he has news to share?"

He shook his head. "Not necessarily. And if you were smart you wouldn't interrogate him, or it may be another three or four weeks before you see him again."

She smacked his arm and he feigned pain. "Ouch!" he howled.

She looked out the window as the buildings floated by. "Okay. I will be happy to spend the evening with our wonderful son, regardless of whether he has big news or not."

A few minutes later, they pulled up to Winston's cottage, parking in the driveway. Winston met them at the door. "Hello, parents," he said warmly. He stepped back. "Come on in."

She gave his arm a squeeze and his cheek a kiss as she passed by him. The moment she stepped inside the familiar living room, however, something struck her. Something different. She sniffed. That was it. The smell of the place. It was cleanser.

"Smells clean in here!" she turned to Winston.

"And how does it look?" he asked with a smile.

She spun back and made visual inspection of the room. She whooped. "You cleaned!" She ran her finger over his entertainment center, normally covered with a thick coating of dust. Clean. She looked at the floors. Clean. Corners? Clean. She ran to the kitchen. "Oh Winston!"

He came up behind her, laughing. "You never thought you'd see the day, right?"

She pulled him into a tight hug. "It looks marvelous." All that nagging paid off, she thought, but didn't say.

"Yep." He turned to the dining table. "Are you guys hungry?"

"You know I am," said James.

The dining room table was neatly set with three placemats, dishes and napkins. On one end sat two closed pizza boxes.

"I got pizza for us. After the shock of the clean house I didn't want Mom to have a heart attack over a home-cooked meal too."

She laughed and they all sat and ate. They talked about Winston's job, Rebel, who was currently in the bedroom with the door closed to allow for a peaceful dinner, and Dad's job. Eventually the conversation circled back to the transformation Winston had given his house.

"What prompted you to do this cleaning all at once?" she asked, working on her second slice of pizza.

Winston drew a breath. He laid down the slice he was eating and folded his hands. "Okay. The clean house isn't the only surprise I have for you tonight."

Lily gasped and looked at her husband. "Told ya."

James' eyebrows drew together. "Let the man speak."

Winston looked at them both, the corners of his eyes crinkling. "I guess you could say the two surprises go together. Well, one leads directly to the other."

Lily wished he would just get to it.

"I'm seeing someone."

She let out a squeal. She'd had a solid idea what the surprise was. Of course, she knew behind the scenes that he'd at least had a few dates with Rose's match. But neither of them had any idea if it had worked out. "Oh, sweetie! Tell us everything. How'd you meet her? What's her name? What's she like?"

Winston gave an amused expression of tolerance. "Mother, I will tell you a little bit, but you will have the chance to get to know her yourself. I'd like the four of us to go out to dinner this weekend."

Lily beamed. "Winston, this is fantastic. I'm so excited for you."

"I met her at a dog park. She's a dog lover like me, and she has a German Shepherd. Her name is Tina Mitchell. She works at a vet's office and is studying to become a vet herself. And she's ... amazing."

James reached out a hand and patted his son's arm. "Glad to hear it, son. Work out the details with your mother and we'll be happy to meet her. Now, isn't there a basketball game on tonight? Want to watch it?"

Lily watched Winston and James make their way to the living room. "I'll clean up the dishes," she called, waving them on. While she cleared the table, her heart raced for Winston. What a happy time in his life. She wished nothing but the best for him and Tina.

And she couldn't wait to tell Rose and Dahlia.

• • • •

THE NEXT AFTERNOON, Lily put on her oven mitt and pulled out a sheet of chocolate chip cookies. The aroma filled her senses, and her stomach growled, anxious for a taste. Laying them on the stovetop to cool, she put three glasses of ice on a tray, a pitcher of sweet tea, three bottles of water and a small bowl filled with lemon wedges. She placed the tray on the kitchen island, along with a short stack of napkins. Last, she scooped the warm cookies onto a plate and placed it near the drinks.

She was ready.

The doorbell rang and there on her front porch stood both Dahlia and Rose. They were talking but looked up at Lily. "Hello! We pulled up at exactly the same time."

"So glad you could make it. Thanks for coming." They came in and Lily collected their jackets. "Help yourself to drinks and cookies."

The ladies gathered in the sitting room with their snacks. While Rose and Dahlia chatted, Lily's excitement level rose. If she didn't tell her friends the good news soon, she felt sure she would explode.

"Could I call the Matchmaking Moms to order?" she interrupted. They looked over at her, surprise showing on their faces. "I'm sorry but I have good news to share."

"What? What?"

Lily grinned. Suddenly speechless, she turned her gaze from Dahlia to Rose. "Rose, you're a genius."

The ladies exploded with enthusiasm. The room filled with squeals and laughter.

"Winston invited James and me over last night. He didn't tell us why, but I knew something was up. The first thing I noticed was his house. It. Was. Spotless!"

Rose said, "Well, that's because he has a new lady in his life, and he wants to impress her."

"And that was the second bit of news. He wants us to meet Tina this weekend."

They reached out and grabbed hands.

"Rose, you did it. You found the perfect woman for Winston and he wants us to meet her."

"Congratulations, both of you," murmured Dahlia.

"We're doing it," Lily said. "We're really doing this thing. Matchmaking Moms rock!"

"Who's next?" Rose asked.

"So, is this one in the can?" Dahlia asked. "When do we know when we're done?"

Lily shrugged. "After I meet Tina and spend a little time with her why don't I report back? If they seem happy and I don't recognize any big red flags to them being together, I'd say our first matchmaking project is done!"

Dahlia tapped her chin. "Okay, so the mother meets the match and we call it done. I have another idea, sort of eye wink to the Matchmaking Moms team. When the mom meets the match, she presents a flower to the couple. Since Rose was Winston's matchmaker, Lily, you'll give Tina a rose. Does that sound fun?"

Lily beamed. "I like that. Sneaky." She nodded. "So, assuming Winston and Tina are solid, who's our next match?"

Dahlia held a notebook in her hand and flipped back a few pages. "According to our planning notes, our second project is Rose's daughter Isabelle and I'll be the matchmaker." She looked up with a strange look on her face. "I just had an idea. What do you ladies say we make this a little more interesting?"

Lily looked at Rose. "What did you have in mind?"

Dahlia tapped her pen against the notebook. "Rose kicked us off and knocked it out of the park. She found Winston a match and he's already introducing her to his parents."

Rose smiled, her cheeks turning pink.

"When did you start your match work, Rose? Four weeks ago? Five? I suggest we add a little wager to the next two matches. Whoever makes a successful match the fastest, wins."

"Wins what?"

Dahlia shook her hand in the air like she was erasing an invisible chalk board. "We can work through all the details till we agree. But are you both open to the concept of making this a little more competitive?"

Discussion followed, but in the end, none of the Matchmaking Moms minded upping the stakes by adding a level of competition.

"Rose has set the bar pretty high. The wager will be the timeline between the first work by the matchmaker and the couple meeting with the parents. Whoever's match does that the fastest, that matchmaker wins. Anything she wants. A gift, an outing, you name it. Within a reasonable dollar amount, of course. The other two matchmakers deliver."

Dahlia and Rose stayed long enough to enjoy sweet tea and cookies. As Lily walked them to the door and they said their goodbyes, she said a silent, *Thank you, Lord. Thank you for introducing me to these women. Thank you for the joy friendship brings to our lives.*

Chapter Seventeen: Tina Meets the Parents

WINSTON GRABBED HIS car keys from the wooden bowl sitting on a table by the door. Gone were the days of searching a half dozen places before finally remembering where he'd placed his keys. His mom's advice came through for him again. Get in the habit of putting them here when he came in. Then they'll always be there when he needed them to go out.

He drew a shaky breath. Nerves were attacking his esophagus and air pipe, making it difficult to breathe normally. He shook out his arms. Get a grip, he told himself. No need for nerves. Tina was a catch, and his parents were happy for him. What could possibly go wrong?

He couldn't help laughing at that thought. Of course, a million things could go wrong. He hoped they wouldn't, however, he didn't have any experience in this situation. Other than a few dance dates back in high school, he'd never introduced a woman he was interested in to his parents, with the hope that they would get along, not just for the evening, but potentially ... just maybe ... for a very long time to come.

That was a lot of pressure to place on a simple dinner out.

He locked up the house and got in the car, starting the drive to Tina's. One other topic nudged his nerves, one that had been bothering him lately. In all their conversations, he'd learned a great deal about Tina, and she'd learned a great deal about him. She'd shared with him that she'd made some bad decisions in college regarding men, and she'd sought forgiveness from God, and was now seeking reformation in her life. Still, she was suspicious of males in general, and tended to jump to the worst conclusions about them.

Although he understood what she was saying, he didn't see it in action, at least, not with him. She tended to be a little hard on herself. Her past relationships didn't come into play between the two of them. All he wanted was for her to be honest with him and let the dynamics between the two of them flow naturally. He liked where their relationship was going.

But that's where he ran into a tiny roadblock. Just as he wanted her honesty, she wanted his. And he had been entirely honest about his past and his hopes for the future. Except for one thing. And that was his gaming habit.

It wasn't a big deal. It wasn't like he was hiding a felony record or anything. It was just a hobby, something he'd enjoyed for years and years to fill his empty hours. Now, he was moving on. He'd missed several evenings of gaming over the last few weeks because he was either with Tina, or he was busy doing something else. Although in the past he could recognize that he was *addicted* to gaming, that wasn't true anymore. Who knows, maybe someday he'd give it up all together.

He should tell her. But something stopped him. Probably her disapproval. He knew she wouldn't be supportive of a hobby that took up so many hours a week online. And why should he upset her with it when he was most likely quitting soon anyway? It didn't impact their relationship.

A Bible verse floated into his mind. Although he hadn't been spending enough time in the Word lately, he must've memorized this one as a child and it seemed to apply to his current line of thought: *"When I was a child, I spoke as a child, I understood as a child, I thought as a child. But when I became a man, I put away childish things."*

His gaming habit was a childish thing. He was a man now, with a job, a house and a relationship. He needed to put it away.

He arrived at Tina's apartment and made his way to her front door. After ringing her doorbell, he pushed the subject out of his mind. It wouldn't come up in their conversation tonight, and he needed to be fully present for this first meeting with his parents.

The door opened and his heart took over, and his mind forgot. Tina had dressed up, wearing a teal green sweater dress and ankle boots, a colorful scarf draped around her neck and her long hair down and shiny.

She looked like a model straight off the runway.

"Wow," he said, drawn out. He pulled her into his arms. "You look absolutely gorgeous, Miss Mitchell."

She giggled into his neck and relaxed into his embrace. "Well, let me see you, Mr. Adams. Because I bet the same could be said for you."

He released her with a smile. She made a show of inspecting him, eyebrows up. "Yes, I do say. You look gorgeous yourself, Mister."

He shrugged and joked, "This old thing?" He'd taken a little more care with his clothes than usual, wearing a new pair of brown denim jeans and a lined dress shirt, untucked.

"Come on in," she said. He followed her into her cozy living room. Max laid there in his dog bed, his tail thumping against the floor.

"Hey Max, buddy. How are you feeling?" He knelt and took the dog's head in his hands.

"He's doing much better," Tina replied. "It's still hard for him to pull himself to his feet with the cast, but once he's up he walks pretty well."

"Good job, Max. You'll be out of that thing soon." He gave him a last tap on the head and stood.

He glanced over at Tina. "You ready?"

She raised a brow. "I suppose. Do you ... do you think they'll like me?"

His heart flooded with affection for her. Why would she be feeling insecure? He stepped closer to her. "Yes, are you kidding? They will not only like you. They'll love you! They were so happy when I told them we were dating. They can't wait to meet you."

"But what if they don't think I'm good for you?"

He held back, shaking his head in disbelief. Although he couldn't imagine this sentiment coming from such a confident woman, he realized to her, it was a real concern. "First of all, they will know you're good for me. They already know, in fact. They've seen differences in me already that can only be attributed to you."

"Really? What?" She sounded dubious.

"Well, I've turned over a new leaf regarding the cleanliness of my house. I admit I was a bit of a slob. But I didn't want to be embarrassed by my messiness when you came to visit, so I cleaned it. And, I've resolved to keep it clean. That – I attribute to you."

She gave him a happy smile. "Aw. You didn't tell me."

He shrugged. "And, I bought some new clothes. Perusing my closet, I realized most of my clothes were at least five years old. I decided to freshen it up a little. Believe me, my mom noticed. She figures you had something to do with that too."

"I didn't. I would've taken you shopping if you asked." Her mouth curved into a smile. "You want to look nice for me?"

"Yeah. Yeah, I do."

She put her hands on his shoulders and pulled him in for a kiss. "Thank you," she whispered. He knew he had put her at ease and now she could be more confident meeting his parents.

Fifteen minutes later, they pulled into the parking lot of a newish seafood restaurant on Ocean Boulevard in Surfside Beach. Mom had suggested it. A white wooden staircase led up to the front door on the second floor. He spotted his parents, already seated. He lifted a hand and made his way over, the other hand on the small of Tina's back. His dad was his usual casual self, but he could tell his mother was beaming over-exaggeratedly. He stifled a chuckle. The poor woman couldn't help herself. Him introducing her to a special someone was a dream come true for her.

"It's such a pleasure to meet you," his mom said as the two women shook hands. His dad joined in with more of a back pat. Tina, obviously thrilled with the warm welcome, gushed her happy sentiments.

They settled in at the table and chatted easily until the waitress came, which reminded them that none of them had looked at the menu. They quieted for a moment while they made their selections, which they gave to the waitress upon return.

If Winston would've had to report back on all the conversation topics after the dinner was over, he would've been sorely unable. They started out with dogs, since that was how he and Tina had met. They moved logically to her job at the vet's office and her schooling to be a vet herself.

After that, his eyes went a little blurry and his attention faded. He believed it was the compliment his mother gave Tina on her dress, which then expanded to where she liked to shop for clothes. Then somehow, they discovered they were members of the same sorority in college, although decades between. When he was finishing his dinner, they had moved on to which music groups they both liked, and which ones they had in common.

More words had been spoken over the last hour and a half in his presence than on any day that he could remember, but he himself had only contributed a handful of them. The two women were talking like they were best friends for life. At one point, Mom pulled a single red rose out of her purse and handed it to Tina. Winston frowned, wondering if that behavior was a little over the top, but Tina accepted it graciously and thanked her.

He shrugged internally. Who knew what women considered good or bad? Probably he'd never fully figure it out.

He glanced over at his dad, who had already been staring at him, waiting to meet eyes. His dad gave him an expression that spoke volumes, shook his head with a close-mouthed grin and looked down at his plate.

After dinner and a walk on the beach, they parted, and Winston drove back to Tina's place. He didn't even have to ask, "How'd you like my parents?" because Tina couldn't stop talking about them, especially his mom. "She is so nice, Winston, and so friendly. She made me feel so welcome. Easy to talk to. Can talk about anything. And they have such a long-term, strong marriage; that's just awesome. And your dad was nice too. Quiet, but warm and loving. You can tell he adores your mom. In fact, you take after your dad, did you know that? Both in looks as well as personality. And your mom's personality is a total opposite, but they just blend so well together, do you know what I mean?"

She looked over at him and he saw his opening. "Yeah. She's more the talker. He's quieter, but they go well together."

He glanced at her and she was happily nodding her head.

He parked and they made their way to her front door, with plans to hang out with Max a little bit. Winston's phone notification sounded. He had a text. He pulled it out of his pocket while Tina worked on her door lock. Glancing down, he saw it was from his mom: "*We love her! She's a keeper, Winston.*" With a thumbs-up emoji. He let out a soft laugh.

"What is it?" Tina asked.

He looked at her, then the phone. Why not show her? He held out his phone so she could read it. Her face told him she loved what she'd read. She stepped into his arms and they stood quietly hugging. "You're a keeper too," she whispered.

Chapter Eighteen: Leia Lands a Big Surprise

TINA DROVE OVER TO Winston's house the next morning. She'd had an awesome time last night. His confession that he was making some changes in his life in order to make room for her had made her heart bloom. Evidently, he'd been a confirmed bachelor and hadn't dated much before her. Knowing him as she did now, she couldn't imagine why other girls hadn't snatched him up. He was not only handsome, he was kind, friendly, considerate. He came from a great family. He had a good career, was self-sufficient. He was always up for whatever activities she suggested, and he also took the trouble to plan good dates himself.

Whatever reason he was still on the dating market, she couldn't care less because it meant he was available for her. And his admission that he'd been paying more attention to the appearance of himself and his house, because he wanted her to be pleased ... that was super good news.

Then, his parents. What delightful people. Regardless of the age difference, she could honestly see herself being friends with Lily. She was fun, positive, upbeat.

And they liked her.

When Winston was preparing to leave last night, she'd invited him to church with her. Although he was a Christian, he hadn't been active at church for some time. She could understand that, she truly could. Many single people of her generation had strayed away from organized religion and hadn't made their way back after college or getting a job. But the key was ... he was willing. He didn't turn his nose up at church and refuse to go. When she'd invited him, he'd said yes. Just like she wanted him to.

She'd offered to drive because it was only fair after he'd driven the night before. But she came a few minutes early because she wanted to check out this place where he'd turned over a new leaf. She was curious to see it.

And why not? She was his girlfriend.

The thought made a happy smile jump on her face. She had a boyfriend. And it was Winston, one of the best.

She walked up to his door and rang the doorbell. Inside, she heard big feet pounding on the floor and Winston shouting Rebel's name. She giggled. When the door swung open, Winston was bent at the waist, holding onto the dog's collar. "Sorry," he said breathlessly. "She's a little crazy this morning. Come on in. If you dare."

She laughed. "Hey Rebel, good to see you, girl." When Winston released her, the big lab made wide circles around Tina, sweeping against her legs, jumping up onto the couch, down again, around and around. In her mouth she held a deer antler, her favorite chew toy. Whenever Rebel swept by her, Tina bent and stroked her back. Finally, the dog calmed, giving Tina the opportunity to glance around.

FINDING LOVE FOR THE LONER 161

They stood in a living room containing a couch, two comfy chairs and a couple side tables. Along one wall sat an entertainment center holding a large television and stacks of DVDs in plastic covers. The walls were a dark green and the floors were gleaming hard wood. Minimal decorations hung but sitting on a shelf were framed photos of Winston with his family.

She turned and saw Winston watching her. "What do you think?" he asked.

"I love it! Very bachelor. Dark walls, leather, wood. Very nice."

He smiled, pleased at her response. "Want to see the rest?"

She nodded enthusiastically and he led her around. It was small, but it was perfect for a single person. It could probably accommodate another adult, she thought giddily, if the need ever arose. A doorway led from the living room to the dining room, which contained a wooden table that sat four, and a sidebar for storage. Another doorway led to a nice-sized kitchen, especially for a house built in the 1940s. It was the same size as the dining room, and many houses made in that era featured teeny tiny kitchens.

A door led out to the fenced-in backyard which was great for Rebel. Another door led to a kitchen pantry and a third door led down to a basement. On the far side of the living room were stairs that led up to three bedrooms and a bathroom. The shower had been recently renovated. The master bedroom was a nice size, and the other two rooms diminished in size.

"That's it," Winston said as they returned to the main room. "It was plenty big enough before I got Rebel. She makes it seem very cramped."

"It's really nice. And I wouldn't say it's cramped. I'd use the word cozy." She smiled up at him. "I love it."

He squeezed her hands. "Let me get my coat. Might need it this morning." While he walked over to the coat closet in the corner, Tina turned her attention to the stack of movies on the entertainment center. "Do you have any movies we might watch together?" She fingered through some.

"Do you like Star Wars? Harry Potter? Lord of the Rings? I have entire series of all those."

"Maybe," she said. Translation: although she wouldn't necessarily pick any of those movies out for herself, snuggling under a blanket with Winston chomping on popcorn with Rebel and Max lying on the floor made the prospect of Movie Night much more attractive.

She reached a stack of plastic covers that each had a label on them: Win4U. She read it aloud and glanced over at Winston. "What's that?"

Curiously, he froze while zipping his jacket. "Oh, um, that's nothing. Just an old nickname. Nobody really calls me that anymore."

"Oh." She shrugged.

"We should probably get going, huh?" Winston suggested. "Don't want to be late for church."

"Oh, yeah, of course." They left the house, Winston locking up behind. In her car, she explained she wanted to introduce him to her friend Becky at church.

"Great. I look forward to meeting your friends."

An emotion flushed through her heart. If she didn't know better, she'd call it love. But was it possible to love someone you'd only known for a month? Or would that be called puppy love? Regardless, she was enjoying her time with Winston, and with God leading the way in their relationship, she felt confident that they had nothing but good things ahead of them.

A few minutes later, they walked hand in hand into Marsh Community Church. She led him to the sanctuary, and they sat. The service commenced and they joined in the singing led by the worship band. Then Pastor went into the Bible passage and his sermon. It was a strong message about character and how you should be comfortable being true to yourself in your dealings with other people. If someone judged you based on your true beliefs, then let them go. It wasn't your job to make everyone like you.

The accompanying Bible verse talked about how perseverance to suffering produced character, and character produced hope in God's love. She loved how Pastor picked relevant topics to feature every Sunday. They gave her something to ponder throughout her week.

She glanced up at Winston and he appeared to be paying attention, entranced by Pastor's words. Her eyes sparkled at him. She would glean his thoughts on the message later.

After church they filed out of the sanctuary and she led him to the coffee table. Fortunately, Winston was a coffee fan and he poured himself a cup of the dark roast. While she was pouring her own, Becky tapped her arm. "Hey," her friend said.

She turned to her. "Hi. I have someone I want you to meet."

Becky's mouth formed a comic "O" and Tina nudged her. "Winston, this is my friend Becky. Becky, Winston."

Becky twirled around and recovered nicely by holding out a hand, shaking Winston's and saying, "So nice to meet you, Winston."

They took their coffees and huddled in a corner where they got a break from the crowd. "I told Becky about you," Tina said to Winston, "and she was looking forward to meeting you."

"Yes, I was," Becky said. "Gotta meet the man who's spending so much time with my best bud here."

Tina rolled her eyes at Winston, hoping Becky wasn't making him uncomfortable.

Winston pulled out a couple conversation starters to engage Becky. Where she was from. What she did for a living. Did she have any kids. The standard, but little did he know that's all it took to get talkative Becky going strong. She did stop occasionally and ask him questions, and before she knew it, her best buddy and her best guy were talking steadily.

Until Winston's phone rang. He pulled it out of his pocket and glanced at it. Then he blanched and stared at it hard.

"Everything okay?" she asked quietly.

"Yeah. No, I'll let it go to voicemail." He stuffed the phone back in his pocket, but his expression was now a worried stone face, and Tina couldn't help but notice, his conversation had come to a fast stop. Becky noticed it too. She turned to Tina and started telling her about something funny that had happened at work last week.

Winston's phone rang again. His eyes opened wide and he pulled it out, staring at it again. "You know," he said, looking at Tina, "maybe I better take this after all."

Tina waved a hand. "By all means. Take your time. In fact, Becky, why don't we go to the rest room?"

He answered the phone while they sidled away. When they were out of earshot, Becky said, "Nice going, lady. He's so good-looking. And he's so nice! You found a good one."

Tina smiled. In the restroom, Tina told her friend, "I hope I'm not putting the cart before the horse here, but this feels special. This feels right. He's a good man and I can't help but wonder if God has put the two of us together."

"Oh, Tina! That's so exciting!"

Tina shook her wet hands into the sink and turned toward the paper towel dispenser. "He's got those long-term qualities that I'd be looking for in a husband. He's kind and polite. He's gentle. He's honorable. I trust him to be honest with me."

Becky took her arm and pulled her into a hug. "I'm so happy for you, Tina. You deserve a great guy and all the happiness."

Tina pulled back and smiled at her friend. "He doesn't have a brother, does he?"

"No, he's an only child."

Becky snapped her fingers. "Darn. Best friend then?"

Tina chuckled. "I'll work on it.

• • • •

WINSTON TOOK LONG STRIDES to put some distance between where he had been standing with Tina and her friend, Becky. On the fourth ring, he swiped the phone and said, "Leia? What's up? Is anything wrong?" Considering she'd never called him out of the blue before, he had to assume a problem. But he couldn't imagine what it would be.

"Not wrong," she said, and that voice that always used to knock him off his feet, didn't have the same impact anymore. "Right. Very, very right."

Winston turned his head, scanning for the return of the girls. "Listen, can we talk later? I'm in the middle of something …"

"Our workshop was approved!"

His mouth dropped open.

"I just heard from GamingCon workshop committee. They approved it. Winston? Are you there?"

"Yeah."

"Isn't this great news? I'll get to meet you and spend time with you in person, and we'll get to present our workshop together."

Suddenly he felt a tap on his back. He whirled around.

"Winston? What is it? You look like you just lost your best friend," said Tina.

Chapter Nineteen: Winston's Double Life

Matchmaking Moms of Oceanview Church

WINSTON'S EYES WIDENED. Leia was on the phone, Tina stood right in front of him. He took a breath. "Okay," he said, working to steady his voice. "I'll give you a call later." And he hung up.

Tina looked into his eyes, her concern evident in her eyes. "Bad news? Are you okay?"

"No," he said. "I mean, no, not bad news and yes, I'm okay." He pushed a smile through his nerves and hoped it wasn't a grimace. He glanced from Tina to Becky and back again.

"Oh! Okay. Becky and I were thinking about going out for a late breakfast. Are you up for it?"

He hesitated. He wanted to. Spend more time with Tina and get to know her friend better. But Leia's call had distracted him and he really needed to think about this dilemma he found himself in and decide what to do.

"I'd like to, but I can't. I agreed to do a work-from-home shift starting at noon. Sorry."

Tina nodded. "How about I drop you off at home and then Becky, I'll meet you at the Pancake House?"

Soon they were in the car, and Winston's head was spinning. What was wrong with him? In order to cover up his lying to her about Leia and his gaming prowess, he had just lied to her about working today.

God, guide me. I know this isn't the way.

Vanessa's words came back to him: Just don't blow it. Well, if he wanted a surefire way to blow this relationship, lying to her would do it.

He needed to be honest with her.

"I'm a little worried about you," her voice came from the driver's seat. He startled.

"Why?"

"Ever since you got that phone call you've been distant and worried. Do you want to talk about it?"

He should say yes. He should come clean right now and hope he hadn't done too much damage. He hadn't been honest with her but if he told the truth now, maybe she wouldn't be too furious.

He looked at her. But he couldn't just blurt it out, unprepared. He needed to plan his explanation so he didn't do any further damage. That's what he would do. He would tell her about his gaming habit, the situation with Leia, the commitment to do the conference workshop, and his resolve to stop the gaming all together. But he needed to put some thought into it first.

"Not right now," he said. "But soon, yes. Okay?" He gave her a smile, a genuine one that reflected his affection for her.

She pulled up to his house and put the car in park. "Okay," she said, patting his cheek. "I'm here for you when you're ready. I'm a good listener."

"Yes, you are." He sat and took in the sight of her. "I'll give you a call later."

He stood on his front step and waved as she drove away. He went in and faced the enthusiastic greeting of his dog. "Hello, hello, come on, come on," he said as he made his way to the backyard. While she ran around sniffing, he stood thinking. Dread descended over him like icing over a cake.

He was living a double life, and he needed to end it now. Leia represented the dark side of his life. She idolized him and his gaming prowess. The pedestal she'd placed him on was uncomfortable and unwanted.

Tina represented the light side. She helped him be a better person and she offered him a potential future full of good and love.

He couldn't have both. He didn't want both. He pictured a devil floating above one shoulder and the angel on the other, that old cliché used in cartoons. The gaming world was his devil and his relationship with Tina was his angel. So why was he lying to Tina? And why had he agreed to further interaction with Leia?

Rebel barked and Winston picked up her ball and tossed it. Urgency filled him. He needed to talk to Tina before he ruined this entire thing. And if he did ... he didn't deserve a good relationship in his life.

His phone rang and he answered without looking.

"Hey, Win4U. Good time to talk now?"

Her voice made him stop. He had to talk to her. He couldn't avoid her forever. He schooled his voice to be casual. "Hey Leia, sorry about earlier. I was at church."

"No problem. So, isn't this great? I knew the committee would be thrilled when they saw my proposal. And they were! You are a superstar, you know that?"

He gave an internal sigh. He'd completely read the workshop proposal wrong, and the committee's reaction to it. The fact that they approved the workshop featuring him as the celebrity guest, and that they were excited about it ... another deception on his part. He'd only encouraged Leia to submit under his assumption that it wouldn't pass muster.

Lies. Once you started, they built on top of each other until there was no way out.

"Leia, we need to talk. I'm sorry but I can't do the workshop after all."

A frozen pause seeped through the phone line. Then, Leia's strained voice, "What did you say?"

"There's a lot going on that I can't get into, but I just can't do the workshop. I'm sorry."

"No. No. You can't do this to me. You are the star of this workshop. They wouldn't have accepted it without you. You were my ace in the hole, Winston."

Winston closed his eyes. *Lord, guide me. Show me.*

"I've already booked my flight and my hotel. The conference paid for it. If I cancel, I'll owe them back. And I don't have the money." She was talking faster and faster, her voice ripped with sobs.

"I'm sorry," he murmured.

"I cleared this with you. You gave me the green light. I don't understand why you'd do this to me." She sniffed and Winston could picture her tears.

He'd done this to her. He'd told her to go ahead and submit the workshop and now that it was approved, he was ripping the rug out from under her. In his drive to become a better man for Tina, he was stepping on Leia.

"Okay, okay, Leia, I'm sorry. Listen. We'll do the workshop. Shhh. We'll do it together."

Her voice came to him in a whimper. "You mean it?"

"Yeah. It was wrong of me to backtrack on you. I'm sorry. We'll do it."

What an idiot he was. He was handling both sides of his life wrong – the light and the dark.

He waited on the line while she recovered from her outburst. Although in his imagination he was beginning to see her as the little devil on his shoulder, she wasn't really. She was just a woman who enjoyed playing video games and had thought of a creative way to earn her way to the big conference. It was no big deal. She had asked him to help her, he had agreed. Now he needed to carry out his promise.

So why did the thought of telling Tina about Leia give him a feeling of dread and an upset stomach?

He finalized his plans with Leia, the date and time of their workshop. He hung up and dropped his head into his hands.

Relationships were a complete mystery to him; he had no idea what he was doing. *Don't blow it, don't blow it.* Repeating his prayer, he sat in the quiet, waiting for an answer.

• • • •

LATE AFTERNOON, TINA sat in her living room, petting Max who was chilled out on the couch while she caught up on some television programs. She wasn't expecting anyone, so when there was a knock on the door, she stared at it for a second. Who would be stopping by? She could only think of one person.

She opened the door and sure enough, it was Winston. She loved the fact that he was comfortable enough to drop by uninvited. She greeted him with a hug and a smile. "Come on in."

He sat on the couch beside Max who rolled over onto his back and straightened his legs, reaching high into the air. Winston chuckled. "That's an invitation for a belly rub if I ever saw one," he said, and proceeded to deliver one. He turned to her. "How was breakfast?"

"It was good. I'm a huge omelet fan but haven't mastered making one at home. Whenever I get the chance to go out for breakfast that's usually what I have."

"Sorry to have missed it. I love omelets too."

She reached out and rubbed her fingertips over his hand. He met eyes with her. "Becky and I talked about you," she said teasingly.

"Oh, yeah?"

"She had good things to say about you. She thought you were cute. And nice."

Surprisingly, this news appeared to bother him. He frowned and let out a sigh. "Tina, I have a confession to make."

Dread made a dive-bomb in her stomach. She wanted to hear what he had to tell her, but she almost didn't want to know. She hadn't been in any serious relationships with a man, but she was aware they weren't easy. That there were occasional problems, and they hadn't hit any yet. But she hoped beyond hope that he wasn't about to confess something terrible that they couldn't work through together.

"Okay," she said cautiously.

He sat for a moment, fortifying himself. Then he said, "I'm a gamer." He turned to her. "Do you know what that is?"

"Not really."

"I play online games with people."

"Video games?"

"Yeah. I used to play several, but now I'm focused on one game called Star Battler. It takes place in outer space and opposing teams fly around in aircraft and fight each other."

"Okay," she said.

"I'm a captain of a team of battlers. I come up with the fight plan and lead them into battle."

She blinked, her mind racing. "This is something you enjoy doing? It's your hobby?"

"Yeah. It's been a hobby for a long time. In fact, it's been the main way I spend my time when I'm not working. It's ... a way of life, really."

"Sounds like you've spent a lot of hours doing it."

He nodded. "Way too many to count. I've been thinking lately that I'm done."

"Why are you done?"

Winston looked down at his lap, then up at her. "Being with you has reminded me that there's more to life. More to do, more to accomplish than sitting in front of the TV for hours at night, racking up wins. I want to be free to spend time with you. I want to do more outside, healthy things. Working out, taking walks. And I want to explore the man God wants me to be."

His news brought out a happy smile on her face. "This is great news. All good, positive resolutions. Maybe God wants something different for you. Maybe he has a plan for you that doesn't involve, what's it called, Star Battlers?"

He lifted a hand and cupped her chin. "Will you help me?"

"Of course! How can I help?"

"Just be yourself. Be tolerant of me when I have a misstep. When I slip back into old habits. It might not be easy to quit all together, especially with so many people counting on me."

She frowned. "Who counts on you?"

"My team. My opponents. They expect me to be there. I need to let them know that I'm pulling back."

Tina nodded, studying his face. "But you want to pull back, right? This is your decision?"

He blinked, then nodded. "Yes. It's hard to break old habits, but it's time to put this behind me."

She leaned closer, resting against him. "I'll help you. You and me, together. We're a team." He turned his head and they joined in a kiss that sent a flush through her system. It felt exciting, full of promise. "I'm excited that you want to explore new activities together."

She put an arm around him, enjoying his warmth beside her. She felt his shoulders tense and she looked up at him. "Is there something wrong? Something else you wanted to say?"

His eyes flickered over hers and finally he started to relax. "No, I've said it all. Thanks for understanding."

Chapter Twenty: Life Goes On

Matchmaking Moms of Oceanview Church

AT WORK THE NEXT DAY, Tina stood beside Beth processing lab work. She glanced at her co-worker, wanting to ask a question, while not revealing why she was asking. She looked back at her specimen. She'd make it hypothetical. "Hey Beth, you have teenaged sons, don't you?"

"Yeah, one seventeen and one nineteen." Beth leaned over a vial and marked on it with black marker.

"Do they play online video games?"

Beth nodded. "Yes, they both do. Have for years. A bunch of their friends meet online at a certain time during the evening to play together. For Zach, my college student, it's a way for him to keep in touch with friends from high school while they're spread out all over the country." She glanced up. "Are there any more samples to do?"

Tina handed her a vial of urine from her work stack, and Beth picked up a chemically treated dipstick to perform the test. "Hearing some kids talking about online gaming, it sounds like it could be somewhat addictive. Is that right?"

"Oh, you betcha. I had to put time limits on Zach and Peter when they were younger, or they never would've gotten anything else done. With school and sports, they were busy already. I didn't like them spending night hours on a game that wasn't productive. An hour or two, sure, to unwind or whatever. But any more than that, it seemed destructive."

Tina nodded, trying to focus on the blood sample she was processing. "Do men play online games or is it just boys?"

Beth chuckled. "If a full-grown man played online games all night, I'd have to wonder about his maturity level."

Tina sniffed, a stab in her heart becoming hard to ignore. Beth didn't realize it, but she'd just insulted Tina's man, making her feel the need to stick up for him. "Maybe a man just had fond memories of playing those games as a teen and didn't have any reason to quit."

Beth turned her head. "Who are we talking about?"

"No one!" Maybe Tina's response was too sudden. "I just read an article about addictions and one was video games. I'd never really thought of gaming being addictive, so I figured I'd ask you."

Beth turned back to her work. "I can see where they're addictive if proper time restraints aren't set."

They both finished up their last samples just as the office manager, Gabrielle came in. "Marty was scheduled to handle the Pet Adoption Event this afternoon over at the pet store, but she called in sick. I need one of you to go."

Tina frowned. "What is it?"

"We've partnered with a couple pet rescue shelters in town and whenever they do an adoption event, we try to send someone over to talk to potential adopters about veterinary care, vaccinations, proper food and exercise. Answer questions, hand out fliers. Today between two and five on the sidewalk outside the pet store on Grand Avenue."

FINDING LOVE FOR THE LONER 177

Tina glanced at Beth with eyebrows up. "That sounds fun. I volunteer, unless you want to go, Beth."

Beth waved her hand. "Nah, I'll stay here."

Tina finished out the last hour at the office, then gathered her stuff to head over to the Adoption Event.

• • • •

WINSTON SAT, ULTRA-aware of the time. It was a few minutes before seven in the evening. The time he'd normally be preparing to join a game. The time he'd usually be slipping on his Win4U persona and sliding into his virtual aircraft.

Gaming had been a part of his life for so long, he couldn't remember life before it existed. Sure, the games had evolved as technology had. He could remember his first gaming station back when it was the only one at ToysRUs, begging his parents to buy it for him so he could try it out. Which led to a new version every year for Christmas as a better and faster one came out on the market. As the internet became more prominent in every home, he moved into online gaming – the ability to play with strangers who shared the love of the game. Eventually, Win4U had become a household name because of his strong win record, which simultaneously was a source of pride for him, and a source of embarrassment.

Among his online faceless, nameless friends who played the game, he was proud. He was their leader, the one they all looked up to. Who wouldn't be proud of his accomplishments and celebrity status?

But here, in his real life, he'd never spoken to anyone about it. Not his parents, not his friends. Because the fact that he was a twenty-eight-year-old single man who spent twelve hours a week sitting on his couch playing video games in the dark was not something he was overly keen on sharing. He had enough perspective to know that made him sound like a nerd.

He was grateful that Tina had reacted to his news as positively as she did. She hadn't gaped at him with a look of disgust when he'd told her he was a gamer. Granted, she probably didn't understand the extent of his commitment to the game. But that was okay, because he was pulling back. He'd gained her agreement to help him quit the habit, and he had seen clearly that he needed to move on. His future didn't lie with the game. God was pressing on his heart the need to move on, hopefully, with Tina by his side.

Her response being as positive as it was, he didn't want to push it by telling her the rest of the story. His record, the upcoming workshop he'd agreed to with Leia. She knew enough to understand his goal of quitting, and that it wouldn't be easy for him. That he needed her support.

He logged onto Star Battler, headphones over his ears. Just like a bandage, he needed to rip it off. Enthused greetings filled his ears, causing a rip of sadness to flow through him. But it was all for the best. Change was good, but it was difficult.

"Hey all, I have something to share. Is everybody on?"

His regulars all spoke up, including Leia.

"Okay, listen, I don't want to make this any harder than I have to. But I wanted to announce that I'm retiring from Star Battler."

Murmurs of dissent hit his ears, along with a few gasps and at least one shout.

"Please, please. I want you to know how awesome it's been playing with you, some of you for years. Some of you not so long. I appreciate all your support and your dedication to the game. I wish you all the best moving forward. But I've reached a new stage in my life and I need to free up some hours to make room for something new. Please understand, it has nothing to do with you guys. You are the best team anyone could ask for. So, with my undying gratitude and best wishes for everyone, I bid my farewell."

Vocal chaos hit his ears. He listened only a few seconds, and then he logged off the game, bringing sudden silence. A lonely void filled his head and for a moment, the desire to log back on overwhelmed him. What was he doing? He belonged there. Those were his people. Star Battler was where he was a someone, where everyone looked up to him. He was a hero to some, a leader to all. What was he thinking, giving all that up? Maybe there was another way.

His pulse raced through his veins, and he squeezed his eyes tight. No. He pictured the cartoon devil on his shoulder. The dark side of his life was pulling him there, not the new, positive, light side.

How could he get past this? When he'd examined it from a distance it seemed so right, so easy. But now in the heat of it, it seemed impossible.

Ask for my help.

The words came to his ears as if someone far away had spoken them. "What?" he whispered. He waited. He didn't hear the words again, but he didn't need to. He knew what he'd heard, and he knew who'd said them.

He bowed his head and let his thoughts out through words. "Lord God, help me to make this change in my life. I know it's what You want me to do. It's hard to make change, even when we know it's positive change. I'm too weak to do it on my own. I know Tina's agreed to help me, but Lord, I need You right now."

He ripped the headphones off. He needed to distance himself if he stood the chance of quitting cold turkey. He slid to the floor, on his knees. "Dear Lord," he murmured. "Help me. Please be with me. Help me make these changes in my life."

He stayed kneeling, head bowed, eyes closed, lips moving until the flow of anxiety passed him. Calmness filled his mind. "Thank you, God," he said. "Thank you."

He stood and fell back into his chair, drawing a shaky breath. The first step was done. If he could lean on Him with each hardship, he'd get through this.

His phone rang. He was surprised when he glanced at it that he'd had two missed calls. He'd been so absorbed he hadn't heard them. They were all from Leia. He owed her an explanation after the bombshell he'd just dropped on her. He lifted the phone to his ear. "Hey, Leia."

He didn't expect exuberance in her voice. He assumed she'd try to talk him out of retiring. "Winston! I can't believe it! I'll miss you during the battles, that's for sure."

"Thanks, Leia. But don't worry, I committed to work with you on the GamingCon workshop and I won't leave you out in the cold. I promise."

"Thank you. In fact, your retirement is timely for the workshop. We're going to pull in thousands of interested gamers, making the workshop even more popular than if you were actively playing. This is going to make you a legend, Winston. I couldn't have planned it any better myself."

They talked a few more minutes and hung up, Winston feeling unsettled. His retirement from gaming was going to make him a conference legend? That felt ungodly to him.

Pushing aside his concerns, he repeated the plan in his mind. He'd quit gaming to make himself free to become a better man, a better boyfriend to Tina and a better Christian. Gaming was behind him. He'd carry through on his commitment to Leia so he wouldn't leave her in the lurch.

The future looked bright. He just needed to focus upward.

Chapter Twenty-One: Love Blooms

Matchmaking Moms of Oceanview Church

AS MARCH BLOOMED IN Murrells Inlet, so did the flowers and the warm weather. Tourists wearing bathing suits and carrying golf clubs flocked to the area for spring break. Restaurants grew crowded and Winston and Tina avoided those popular with vacationers. Instead, they either ate out at casual eateries that catered to locals, or they cooked together in his kitchen or hers.

Winston loved the routine they'd developed of seeing each other a few evenings a week, and every weekend. One date he planned, followed by the next date of her planning. This required him to step up his game and not fall into bad habits such as sitting in front of the TV with her each night.

Tonight, he stopped at the grocery store after work and picked up fresh shrimp, scallops, cream, bacon and baby potatoes. He'd found a recipe on a website that sounded good, and he knew with Tina's help, they could make it together for dinner. When he arrived home, he laid all the ingredients on the counter as well as the recipe he'd printed out.

Tina arrived ten minutes after he'd changed clothes into khaki shorts and a soft, well-worn button-up shirt with sleeves rolled up. She walked in without ringing the bell, partially because they were that familiar with each other now, and partially because Rebel grew agitated when the doorbell rang, and this way, the dog could celebrate the surprise of Tina's arrival.

Tina held a stalk of something green in her hand, but he ignored it until after he'd welcomed her by pulling her into his arms, resting his face into the spot where her neck met her shoulder and breathed in her scent. Placing his lips on hers for a quick kiss, he said, "Missed you today."

She smiled happily. "Missed you, too." She shook the greens at him. "I had extra fresh parsley from the last recipe we made so I figured we could chop some and put it in the seafood chowder."

He nodded. "Good. Recipe doesn't call for it but it's always good to improvise."

"I can't wait to get this going." She rubbed her hands and stalked into the kitchen. "I haven't had fresh shellfish in, I don't know how long."

They took their places at his counter, side-by-side, following the recipe, chopping, browning, stirring, until the full chowder was in the stockpot, thickening over a low heat. They both stood and watched it form, their stomachs groaning for that first taste.

Tina turned to look at him. "I know this is your date to plan, but can I go off the rules a tiny bit and suggest something to do after dinner?"

Relief flushed through him because he hadn't planned anything for after dinner. But he gave her a good-natured expression of disappointment. "Well, I guess I'll have to put away the big plans I had for a private concert with your favorite artist. Whatcha got?"

She tilted her head. "And just who, by the way, would my favorite artist be?"

He stilled. "Radley Ray?" he guessed. He figured he was safe picking a popular country artist because she was a huge country fan. She turned on the country station every time she drove, and he'd heard her singing along word for word more times than he could count. But was he her favorite? He'd find out.

She giggled. "Close enough." She punched his shoulder. "Downtown Myrtle Beach, near the carousel, there's a bandstand. Tonight, they have a free debut performance of a new song and dance troupe, starring one of our clients from the vet's office. They're doing Broadway show tunes. I promised her I'd come if I could. You into it?"

He suppressed a moan. Broadway show tunes weren't particularly his cup of tea, however, he could recognize several benefits from going. First of all, he'd be with Tina, which was always good. He'd get brownie points for going. Third, oh heck. Doing anything with Tina along was better than not being with her.

"Sure," he said, and she lifted her hand for a high five.

Ninety minutes later, they had savored their seafood chowder, packaged the leftovers for later, driven downtown, found a parking spot, hiked fifteen minutes to the bandstand, and were now waiting for the performance to begin. The stage sat along the oceanfront, and the audience brought their own seating to set on the sand. Fortunately, Tina had come prepared with a big blanket. After laying it down, they stretched out.

She positioned herself in the V of his outstretched legs, leaning back against him. He wrapped his arms around her and rested his chin on her shoulder. It was cozy. He looked up and down the beach and noticed that this troupe had pulled a pretty good crowd for a weeknight. The sun was beginning its descent and the temperatures were a comfortable shorts-but-sweatshirt level. He took it as his personal responsibility to make sure Tina stayed warm.

He wrapped his arms tighter around her and let his lips wander over her neck. She shivered and sighed.

His mind began to wander to how his life had changed positively over the last three months. Here he sat on the beach with his amazing girlfriend, spending his time in fun and interesting ways. Four months ago, could he have ever imagined an evening like this? Creating new recipes for dinner with a beautiful woman by his side, snuggling on the beach and opening himself up to a show tune revue? No. He'd be doing the same old thing he always did. Stuck in a rut.

Change was good. And the evenings he spent with Tina, he barely had a flicker of regret about not logging on. He rarely thought about his team joining together on the web and playing together, because he had other things, *better* things to do.

Of course, those nights that he wasn't with Tina, he still felt the tug to join them, and the sadness when he resisted. That's when he would pray to God for strength and renewal of his vow.

He was excited about his life. And it was all due to this woman he held in his arms. Before he realized what he was doing, he leaned closer to Tina's ear and said, "I love you, Tina."

His eyes popped open and his heart may have stopped beating for a moment. How would she react? It was true on his part, he was convinced. But was it too soon? Did she not feel that way at all?

Don't blow it, don't blow it.

She turned slowly in his arms so she could see his face. He kept his eyes focused on hers, his heartbeat now pounding in his ears.

"Winston," she said, a smile forming on her face. "I love you too."

He raised his face to the heavens, thanking God silently over and over. She loved him too. Thank you, God.

She turned and grabbed his face and pulled it to hers. She kissed him long and hard, and just when he thought he'd die from not breathing, she released him. He grabbed a deep breath and took in her beauty and the joy etched on her face.

They loved each other. Life was good.

• • • •

TINA BREEZED INTO WORK a few days later, joy for life filling her heart. She greeted her co-workers cheerfully on the way to her locker. Beth was already stationed at the lab table. "Hello," Tina crowed.

Beth looked up with a questioning expression. "Someone's in a good mood lately. What's up with you anyway?"

Tina broke out into a chuckle. "Can't I say hello with a smile on my face without you wondering if something is up?"

Beth laid down her tools and studied Tina as she readied her workstation. "Something's different. Oh. I know."

Tina glanced over at her, then back at her work.

"Did you, how do I say this delicately, reach a milestone with that boyfriend of yours to put that smile on your face?"

Tina knew exactly what she was referring to, and the answer to that particular question was, and would continue to be, *no*, for quite some time. But that intimate knowledge was none of Beth's business.

But coincidentally, she could answer in the positive to that question and mess with Beth's brain a little bit. She worked to hide her amused grin. "In fact, yes, a milestone was reached with Winston for the first time that has given me a whole new lease on life and put a permanent smile on my face."

Beth nodded knowingly but Tina didn't want her to get the wrong idea, so she set her friend straight. "We said we love each other."

"Oh!"

Tina almost laughed out loud, Beth looked so surprised.

"Well, how nice. I'm sure he's a very nice young man."

She nodded. "Yes, he is. A very nice, fun, handsome, honest, godly young man. Just my type." And she turned back to work without any more conversation.

Chapter Twenty-Two: Winston's Last Hurrah

THE DAY OF THE WORKSHOP was fast approaching. Leia had contacted him twice since his retirement announcement, keeping him informed. But honestly, she'd made it easy on him. He simply needed to show up, be introduced, wait till the end of her presentation, then lead them through a few demonstrations projected on the big screen.

He could do it with his eyes closed. It would be easy, but he dreaded it. In the weeks since he'd left the game, he'd found his footing. He'd built a new life, really. And it didn't involve gaming.

Being the celebrity guest at Leia's workshop made him uncomfortable. He felt like an imposer, someone who didn't belong there anymore. And the last thing he wanted was to be pulled back in, when he'd worked so hard to break away.

But leaving Leia out in the cold didn't feel right either. He'd made a commitment, now he just had to carry it out and be done with it forever. In a way, this was a gift from Leia. Everyone dreamed of retiring on a high note. Leia's workshop gave him his high note. Then, *adios*.

He submitted his request at work for the day off. It was approved with no question. Now, he just needed to get through the next few days, show up and do it. And that would be that.

• • • •

TINA SAT ON THE CHURCH pew, wedged between Winston on her left and Becky on her right. The three of them had formed the habit of sitting together during worship services. Winston didn't mind sharing her with Becky, and occasionally, they would go out to brunch together afterward.

After the service, Winston offered to get coffee for the three of them. Tina nodded her thanks, before he walked away. She and Becky secured comfortable easy chairs in the corner.

"Can I just tell you, friend?" Becky said, patting Tina's knee. "You are positively glowing. You look so happy."

Tina had hoped she'd have a chance to confide in her friend her awesome news. She dove in before Winston returned. "We're in love, Becky. We both said it."

Becky let out a whoop, much louder than the setting called for. Tina shushed her aggressively. "Not so loud." Her gaze darted around the room, looking for Winston, glad she didn't see him. "He told me last week and I immediately told him back."

"Awww, buddy, I'm so happy for you. I strongly approve. He's a good guy, and it's clear how much he loves you with every look."

Tina's heart was melting. "We're going to work on you next," she promised.

"I'm going to hold you to that." Becky smiled at her friend. "What's your favorite thing about Winston?"

Tina drew in a deep breath while she ran the question through her mind. "So much. He's just so easy to be with, you know? He's up for anything, he's happy. He's honest. We've had a bunch of conversations and he's gone pretty deep. As I have. I feel like we know pretty much all there is to know about the other. There's no secrets. And we accept each other just as we are."

Winston was approaching, juggling three disposable cups of coffee. Tina put a finger over her lips, hoping to communicate to her friend to keep this revelation between the two of them. She wasn't sure if Winston would be comfortable knowing she was telling everyone they loved each other. But of course, knowing him, he'd probably be fine with it.

Becky got the message. When he sat down, they began a discussion about the sermon points.

• • • •

WINSTON AWOKE HOURS before his alarm, his heart uneasy. Nerves were getting the best of him on this day, the day he'd been waiting for.

Dreading.

Something deep within him was causing this anxiety. Why? He knew he was going down the correct path leaving the game behind. Today's workshop at GamingCon would be his final farewell.

He knew why he was anxious. Because he hadn't told Tina what he was doing today.

He'd told her all about his gaming habit. He'd told her he planned to break the habit. He asked her for help when he felt like going back.

But he hadn't told her he'd be participating in a workshop today as his last activity as a gamer. And since confessing their love for each other, they'd been very open and honest with each other. Why had he withheld this one fact when she'd been so supportive of everything else?

Because she didn't know him as Win4U, super captain of Star Battlers. She knew him only as Winston Adams, boyfriend. After today, Win4U wouldn't exist. So what was the point in bringing her into this world now?

He closed his eyes. *Don't blow it, don't blow it.* Vanessa's words flowed through his mind, as they often did. He was so inexperienced in the art of love, he couldn't trust his instincts. He'd have to rely on God's guidance.

Letting out a pent up breath, he rose, Rebel getting excited in her crate beside his bed. "Hey girl, you up early too? Want to go take a run to get the day going?"

• • • •

TINA ARRIVED AT WORK mid-morning, scheduled for the late shift today. As she made her way past the animals in the waiting room she patted them on the head and gave them each a kind word. She passed through the reception area, greeting her co-workers and headed back to the lab. Her supervisor, Gabrielle, met her there with a sheet of paper in her hand.

"Hey Tina, remember when you did the pet adoption event? How did that go?"

Tina smiled. "Great. I enjoyed it. I talked to the potential adopters about health topics and in between visitors, I played with the dogs."

"I've got another one on the schedule today. Want to go?"

"Sure!"

Gabrielle handed her the paper. "Here's the flyer. Why don't you arrive about noon and head back here around three? It's in Myrtle Beach so it'll be a half hour drive or so."

"Sounds good." Tina turned back to her lab stack as Gabrielle walked away. She was ready to plow through her lab work and then enjoy a little break in the action later at the event.

• • • •

WINSTON DROVE NORTH on Highway 17 toward Myrtle Beach. The two-mile early morning jog with Rebel had calmed him and he was now ready for whatever today presented him. He had received a text from Leia this morning telling him when and where to meet her.

Familiar landmarks passed by outside his window as he drove. When he reached the convention center, he drove into the parking garage and selected a spot. Walking back out to the sidewalk he made his way to the front entrance and stepped inside. He would meet Leia here.

He wondered for a moment what she'd look like. He had a certain image of her in his head, formed by the sound of her voice and the cartoon avatar that accompanied her presence online. She looked like a young Princess Leia from Star Wars. But voices don't always go with appearances. She could look entirely different.

"Winston?" His head jerked toward the voice, and his wondering was over. A young woman stood in front of him, petite and slim. Her hair was dyed a bright yellow color – not blonde, but a sunshine yellow. Her face contained several piercings that drew his fascination. He pulled his gaze away because he didn't want to be rude by staring. She wore denim and leather, calf-length pants and high-top sneakers. He broke out in a smile. She looked just like she should look.

"Yes! Leia?" He held out a hand to shake but as she took it she pulled him into a hug. Afterward, she grinned at him. "I hope you don't mind a hug. I feel like with everything we've been through together, it was warranted."

Winston stammered but pulled himself together quickly. If she'd noticed his awkward moment, she didn't let on.

"I can't tell you how excited I am to be standing here with you. I've been planning this day for months and it's finally here."

Winston nodded. "I'm happy too," he said simply.

She pointed across the street. "I scoped out a diner down the street. We've got about an hour before our workshop. How about we go over there and come up with a game plan?" She hooked her arm through his and they headed for the diner.

• • • •

TINA GPS'D THE ADDRESS of the adoption event. She was familiar with downtown Myrtle Beach, but not intimately so. Approaching the pet store, she realized there was no parking lot. But street parking was scarce. Something was going on in this block because there was a ton of traffic, both cars and foot.

She drove past the store, turned down a side street, went three blocks and found a single open spot on the street. She'd take it, she decided and pulled in. She didn't mind stretching her legs for several blocks.

She parked and pulled out a stack of veterinary flyers that she'd use as handouts. She walked a brisk pace and arrived at the pet store a minute or two late. Locating a woman she recognized from the pet shelter, she said, "I'm here! Sorry I'm late! There's nowhere to park around here."

The woman waved a hand. "Tell me about it. There must be something big going on in the convention center today."

"Hope it doesn't discourage people from attending."

"Me too. Hopefully pet lovers will still show up." She took Tina by the arm and introduced her to the other volunteers and the dogs and cats being featured today. She headed toward a visitor peeking into the dogs' crates, then said over her shoulder, "Thanks for coming."

"No sweat. I fully support the cause of adopting rescue pets." She got busy greeting the dogs.

• • • •

THEY HAD FINISHED THEIR briefing for the workshop. Leia beamed at Winston across the table, causing a slight discomfort to flush his face.

"You are awesome, you know that?" she said way too seriously.

"No, Leia," he said, wanting to set her straight. That he wasn't awesome, that the gaming world wasn't awesome, that there were way more productive ways to spend her time than getting wrapped up into this world. But he couldn't spit out the words. He barely had time to form the thoughts in his head when she interrupted.

"Yes. You are the best Star Battler captain in the history of the game, and you deserve the accolades that you get."

"Leia, look, I'm not comfortable with ..."

But she'd tilted her head up at the approach of someone to their table. Winston turned to look at a man in his mid-twenties wearing a t-shirt featuring a comic book superhero tucked into jeans. Around his neck he wore a lanyard and a nameplate that read "LookyCookie."

"Oh my gosh, is it you?" the man exclaimed. "Win4U? I'm LookyCookie." He stuck out a hand. "So proud to meet you in person."

"Looky," Winston said, coming to his feet and shaking hands. "Nice to meet you, man." They'd played together for several years, and he was a good battler. Although they'd never seen the other's face, and never spoke about anything other than the game, Looky was a comrade in arms.

"Unbelievable," the man gushed. He looked at Leia. "And I presume you're LeiaPower?"

"You bet. Are you coming to our workshop today?"

"Of course. You need to ask? I wouldn't miss it. In fact, there are four more of our team members here in person." Looky rattled off the handle names and Winston felt a pleasing flush of familiarity fill him.

"Well, we don't want to be late," Leia said. They left the diner together.

• • • •

TINA STOOD ON THE SIDEWALK in front of the crates of dogs hoping to find their "fur-ever" homes today. They'd had a small showing since she'd gotten here but that wasn't unusual. All it took was a few interested adopters ready to pull the trigger and the event would be considered a success. She'd just finished sharing vaccination information to a college student who was graduating soon and wanted to celebrate by adopting a dog. But bringing a dog home was not where the responsibility, or cost, ended as a new pet owner. Tina hoped she'd set the expectation accurately without discouraging the girl from adopting.

As she turned to watch the young woman walk toward the dogs, a motion caught the corner of her eye. A gait, a stride. Something familiar, but almost subconscious. Her eye followed and that's when she saw him.

Winston, walking down the block across the street. He was in the center of a threesome, a man and a woman.

She called for him, but the busy traffic prevented him from hearing. She watched him, wondering what he was doing downtown on a workday. And as the oddly dressed young woman slipped her arm into his, clutching his forearm, Tina frowned.

"Winston!" she called again, but she knew he was too far now to hear. She about took off after him, and then she remembered, she was working. She had a job to do here.

"Excuse me, can I ask you a question about kennel cough?" She watched her boyfriend one last moment, noting that he turned with his small entourage into the front entrance of the convention center. Then she dragged her attention away, even as her stomach hit her with an attack of nausea. She turned to an older woman. "Yes, kennel cough. What would you like to know?"

• • • •

FINDING LOVE FOR THE LONER

WINSTON ENTERED THE convention center and immediately spied the large GamingCon banner hanging on the wall behind a registration table. A rush of excitement lit his heart. Leia pulled him past the lines of people to a far table. She approached the worker and said, "Workshop presenters, Leia Hernandez and Winston Adams."

The man turned to a stack of manila envelopes and started walking his fingers through them. "Here we are." He pulled two out and handed one to Leia, one to Winston. "Welcome to GamingCon. Good luck with your workshop."

Leia thanked him and they moved away. "I'm heading to the workshop room now," Looky said. "I want to reserve a good seat."

Leia checked her phone for the time and said, "We have a few minutes. I want to show you something." She tugged on his arm. He followed her, knowing he should ask her to stop leading him around like a dog on a leash, but he was so overwhelmed by the grandeur of the crowds at the conference, he kept quiet.

She stopped and gestured. A massive stand-up banner displayed his own avatar that he'd used for his entire gaming career. In huge letters, "The Unparalleled Rise of Win4U," and in smaller letters, "Star Battler track," the date, time and location of their workshop. His mouth dropped open as he stared.

"Like it?" Leia asked after his silence lasted several moments.

"It's, uh, it's really something."

Leia laughed. "Something ... good or something ... bad?"

Winston had no idea what to say. Those warring characters on his shoulder had appeared again. One was urging him to be excited, to bask in the praise, to accept that he'd earned all the accolades with his own hard work.

The other made him want to cringe. He was sure the Bible taught many lessons about being humble before the Lord. He just hadn't studied the Bible enough to come up with one in this moment. Regardless, this banner and the workshop content were definitely not humble. Not in the least.

Leia was staring at him with a huge smile and he mumbled something, enough to satisfy her, then she said, "Time to get to our workshop."

He pried his arm out from hers.

"Because of the interest level, they put us in a ballroom. We can seat hundreds!" They arrived at the ballroom door and walked in. Breath caught in his throat and Winston stopped, his eyes wide and his chest tight.

"Uh, Leia?" he said softly, but she'd already headed off toward the platform at the front. Many seats were already filled with mostly young men and teens wearing the conference lanyard and name badge around their necks.

Winston stumbled to the front and Leia gestured enthusiastically to him. He made his way up the steps to a makeshift stage. She took the manila envelope out of his hands, opened it and pulled out the lanyard, draping it over his head. He looked at it dumbly. *Win4U. Winston Adams. Star Battler captain. Workshop leader.*

"Hey, you okay?" He turned and Leia was giving him a strange look. "You feel all right?"

He took a few breaths and shook himself out. He needed to get himself together before he did something embarrassing like pass out in front of all these people. "Yeah. Could I get some water?"

She led him to a table. She poured a cup from the pitcher of iced water and gave it to him. "Just leave the hard stuff to me. I'll do your intro, most of the workshop content, and you'll do the demos at the end. Relax. This should be the highlight of your life so far." She stepped away, gathering her notes and placing them on the podium.

No, this was not the highlight of his life so far. He'd had quite a few lately, such as meeting Tina and drawing closer to the Lord. But this one was ending. Soon.

Within a few minutes all the seats in the room were full. More people stood in the back and the sides. Leia looked ecstatic at the turnout, and he was happy that she was happy. She'd worked hard to get here and deserved a successful workshop.

A man climbed up on the stage. He stood in front of the podium and spoke into the microphone. "Welcome to GamingCon. You are currently in the Star Battler workshop track. This one is called The Unparalleled Rise of Win4U. If you didn't intend to be here, you may leave now." He paused and looked up. A murmuring filled the room, but no one left their seat. The man at the microphone chuckled. "I didn't think so."

He introduced Leia and the crowd applauded. She stood, patting his shoulder as she passed by him. At the microphone, she cleared her throat. "My name is Leia Hernandez, but some of you may know me as LeiaPower." The crowd cheered and whistled. "I have the distinct pride and opportunity to present to you, in a moment, the greatest Star Battler captain in our universe. But before I do, let me tell you how I came to be in this unique position."

Winston put his head down, trying to level out the racing of his heart. What was this? Simple nerves from being the center of attention, something he was never comfortable with? Or was it more? *Is that you, Lord*? Was God trying to tell him to get out of there? Unfortunately, he didn't have enough experience with listening to God's voice to know.

He made fists and decided to weather through till the end, just like he planned. He tuned back in, and Leia was covering a bunch of statistics of his gaming career, stuff he didn't even know himself. She was building up to an impressive finish, baiting the crowd. Then he heard it. "And I give to you, Win4U ... Winston Adams!"

He came to his feet and looked out at the crowd, mostly standing, all clapping and some whistling. He forced a smile on his face. Leia was suddenly by his side and she grabbed his wrist and thrust it up into the air. "Yes! Yes!" she yelled, each time thrusting his arm in victory.

He wanted out of there.

But he couldn't do that to Leia. And he couldn't do it to all these people who'd come to see the workshop.

Then a scene from that neglected book emerged from the back of his mind. Jesus riding into Jerusalem on a donkey, the crowds lying palms at the animal's feet, yelling their adoration toward him. They cheered and whistled, just as this crowd was doing.

But he knew what had come after the cheering crowd in that story. Winston shivered and focused on the moment. He pulled his arm back from Leia and waved, then used his hands to calm them, bring them down, so he could turn the workshop over to Leia.

FINDING LOVE FOR THE LONER   201

"Don't worry," Leia said. "You'll get your chance to see Win4U in action and there will be time for questions and answers. Now, have a seat and let's start the workshop."

• • • •

TINA WAITED TILL THE doggie visitors had cleared and told the rescue shelter volunteer that she was taking a short break. At the woman's nod, she took off down the block toward the convention center.

Curiosity had her wondering why Winston was here and what he was doing. Did he have some part in whatever was happening inside the convention center? Was he attending because of his job?

One way to find out. Just inside the front door, she was drawn to the registration table and the massive banner. GamingCon?

So, this didn't sound like a work conference. Winston had told her he used to be an avid online gamer. But she was quite sure he'd quit. She'd have to ask him about it the next time she saw him.

She turned and was heading back toward the door, when she caught something familiar out of the corner of her eye. She turned and walked to a stand-up banner. Something about the wording ... Win4U. Where had she heard that before?

She pondered on it a moment, then her eyes popped open in recognition. She'd seen Win4U inside Winston's house the first time he'd invited her over. She studied the illustration on the banner, a vicious-looking cartoon character wearing a metal spiked helmet, holding an airplane's steering device. Then wording: *The Unparalleled Rise of Win4U, inside the ballroom.*

It was a conference workshop, she realized. She noted the date and time. It was happening right now.

Best way to get to the bottom of this puzzle was to go there. Maybe Winston was inside.

She walked the short distance to the ballroom entrance and slipped inside. She gazed around the room. There must be hundreds of people here. Most were standing. All were cheering.

She craned her neck to see what they were cheering at. Unable to see over their heads, she walked to the side to get a better view of the front.

Her mouth dropped open and her breath slowed in her throat.

Winston stood on the stage alongside that odd woman she'd seen him walking with earlier. She was holding his arm up in the air, pumping it excitedly as the crowd yelled. What on earth was going on?

Tina stared, wide-eyed, while the applause came to a gradual stop. Winston sat while the woman spoke. It was easy to tell that the woman admired him, that she looked up to him. She spoke with such passion and gazed at him with stars in her eyes.

She stayed long enough to hear the woman use words such as "unparalleled," "magnificent" and "epic." And her heart sank.

This was Winston she was talking about. *Her* Winston. The Winston she had just professed her love to. The one she'd thought was so different from her other failed relationships.

The Winston she'd sworn was humble and honest and open. The one she'd thought always told her the truth.

Instead …

Sitting up there on that stage was some unrecognizable Winston. A man who soaked in the glory of adorers. Hundreds of fans stood on their feet and cheered for him. She had no idea how to process that.

Why hadn't he told her?

Not telling her something that was such a big part of his life ... that was a lie, wasn't it?

He'd lied to her. And if he'd lied to her about something this big, what else was untrue about him?

Did she really even know him at all?

She turned to the door and slipped out.

Chapter Twenty-Three: No Time for Winston

TINA STUMBLED OUT OF the convention center, crossed the street and made her way back to the adoption event on the sidewalk. She approached the rescue shelter volunteer. "I'm not feeling well. I need to leave."

The woman glanced at her with concern. "Oh my, you look pale. Do you need a ride? You probably shouldn't be driving."

But all Tina could think of was escape. She had to get out of there. "No thank you, I'm fine. I'm sorry."

She waved a hand. "No trouble at all! Take care."

It was a miracle she remembered where she'd parked her car, but she found it and sat in the driver's seat, her breath rushed. Tears threatened her eyes, but she knew she needed to hold it together enough to call Gabrielle at work.

She dialed and placed the call. "Gabrielle? I'm so sorry. I suddenly don't feel well. I need to get home and rest."

Gabrielle was kind, suggesting it was a flu bug, and Tina didn't correct her.

"Hopefully I'll be back in tomorrow."

After she hung up, the tears threatened again, but she couldn't allow them. She had to remove herself from this place. She started her car and left.

• • • •

THE WORKSHOP WAS OVER. Winston stayed and shook hands with every last attender. He signed flyers, he posed for selfies, he answered questions. Now, he was done.

While the convention center crew cleaned up the empty room, preparing it for the next workshop, Leia walked him to the door. She turned to him and lingered. "I can't thank you enough. You made all this possible for me. You're amazing."

He shook his head. "I'm glad it worked out." He took a breath. "Enjoy the rest of the conference."

She smiled and rattled off the other workshops she was excited about and Winston realized not a single one held any interest for him. One day, yes, he'd been in the fan group. But not now.

"Stay in touch," Leia said in that deep voice that had once drawn him.

He knew he wouldn't. He waved and walked out.

• • • •

WHEN SHE'D DRIVEN ALL the way home and let herself into her apartment, Tina finally allowed the tears to fall. She went to her bedroom, pulled off her outer clothes and plopped into bed, sobs heaving her chest.

She cried loudly for a good thirty minutes, and then her tears dried but her sadness remained.

Winston had betrayed her by not confiding in her the extent of his gaming involvement. He evidently wasn't just a gamer. He was a gaming legend. Why wouldn't he tell her that? And if it was true that he was quitting the game, why would he be the star celebrity at Gaming Con, drawing the cheers and praise of hundreds of people?

It just didn't make sense.

She closed her eyes. It was happening again. She simply didn't have good judgement skills when it came to selecting men to date. All of her dating relationships had been disasters.

She'd thought Winston was different. She was so sure of it. She'd entrusted her heart to him; she'd fallen in love. She'd never done that before.

She was so sure, and yet, she was so wrong. Obviously, she couldn't trust her selections when it came to men. Was she destined to be single her entire life? If she couldn't trust Winston, could she ever trust anyone?

She closed her eyes and pulled the blanket over her head.

• • • •

WINSTON HAD A LIGHTNESS in his step and in his heart as he left the convention center. He was done with gaming, and he'd ended that chapter of his life in an epic way. He'd left all those other workshops behind without a single craving to attend them. If he'd been addicted to online gaming before, he felt certain he no longer was.

He returned home and spent the rest of the day with Rebel, throwing balls in the backyard, taking her for a long three-mile walk, lounging on the couch with her while he watched a movie. He sent Tina a couple texts, wondering if she had time to get together this evening but she never responded. Then he remembered she was working the late shift and wouldn't be off till seven.

FINDING LOVE FOR THE LONER

He put together a dinner for himself and Rebel, and at seven thirty he called Tina. No answer. This caused him a little concern. Even when she was busy, she'd try to take a few seconds to return texts. And she rarely missed a phone call.

Maybe she needed help? He closed Rebel in the house and headed over to her place. Just a quick wellness check. If she didn't have time to spend together tonight, that was fine. But he needed to see for himself that she was okay.

• • • •

TINA'S DOORBELL RANG and it was easy to ignore it. She wasn't up for company, she didn't want to make pleasant chitchat and she looked horrible after an afternoon spent crying.

Then it rang again, accompanied by a knock. The person was persistent, and that gave her a clue as to who it was.

Next, another knock and a voice. "Tina? Are you in there? It's me. Are you okay?"

She blinked. She considered staying silent until he went away. She needed peace tonight. On the other hand, he would only come back. Tomorrow or another day. She needed to face him. To talk this out and see what he had to say.

She dragged herself to her feet and pulled open the door.

His eyes widened at the sight of her. She could imagine how horrible she looked but she didn't care. She left the door open and trudged to the couch.

He followed her, closing the door quietly. "Tina, what's wrong? Are you okay? Did something happen?"

She looked at him long and hard and he sank down on the couch beside her. "Oh yes, something happened, Winston."

She rubbed a hand over her cheek, long stripped of makeup by her tears. "In fact, why don't you tell me what happened? Today? At the convention center?"

That comment gave him pause. She could see the shock on his face, the dread in his eyes. Then, in a small voice, "You were there?"

"Yes. Yes, I was there, along with hundreds of your adoring fans, Winston. And your huge banner with some horrid-looking cartoon character that was, what? Supposed to be you?" She couldn't help getting angry and loud and accusatory. It was in her nature, after all. It was one of the many reasons she'd never been successful at love in the past, because when she was hurt or confused, she always struck out and attacked. Well, he deserved it.

"Okay, let me explain," he said, his eyes darting between both of hers.

"You lied to me."

"Yes, I did. I'm sorry, I ..."

"I thought you were different. I see I was wrong."

"Give me a minute. Let's just talk about this."

"I can't. Not tonight. It's too ... raw."

His eyes scanned her face, realization dawning. "Have you been crying? Because you saw me at the workshop?"

She hated admitting that she'd been that weak. That she'd let him upset her that much. She was stronger than this. On the other hand, it gave her a small sense of pleasure letting him know just how much he'd hurt her with his lies.

She didn't have to answer because he knew her that well. He reached for her hands, but she pulled them back.

"I'm sorry, Tina. Really. I didn't mean for you to be hurt."

FINDING LOVE FOR THE LONER

"Because you didn't mean for me to find out?"

His head bowed so she knew she'd hit it on the mark. "You can go, Winston."

He shook his head. "No, let's talk about this. I made a mistake. You need to know why."

"Not now. I need to get over this on my own." Like she always had. Like she probably always would.

"No, not alone. Together. I love you, Tina. Let me apologize."

Her heart started to melt with tenderness for him, but she wouldn't allow it. He couldn't lie to her and get away with it. She stood up and walked to the door, opened it and turned in his direction.

He sat motionless, then hung his head. Getting to his feet, he came to the door. "Tina, I didn't mean to hurt you. I'm sorry you were there to see all that."

She nodded and looked down, examining her bare feet. "I thought you were different from the other guys, Winston. But I was wrong."

Her words stopped him. He took a breath and turned to leave. Then he turned back. "Give me a chance to show you how sorry I am. Not now, but once you're feeling better. Don't throw everything we have away, okay? Will you promise me that?"

Tears stung her eyes again, and she couldn't imagine that another ounce of water existed in her body. "I think it's you who threw everything away, Winston." And she shut the door, turned the dead bolt and shoved Winston out of her heart.

• • • •

HE HAD NO IDEA HOW he got home because now, an hour later, he had no memory of it. His head was a blur, his emotions shut down. Vanessa's advice was on a continuous loop running through his mind. As much as he'd tried to follow it, it appeared that he had, in fact, blew it.

No wonder, really. He was a loner. He'd never had a serious relationship before, and he had no idea what he was doing.

He should've told her about Win4U and risked her anger over his lifestyle choices. She may have walked away then, but by hiding it, she now felt lied to. And she'd walked away anyway.

He was alone again. He should be used to it.

But he wasn't. Not anymore. He'd had a taste of love and he wanted it back. He was in love with Tina, body and soul, and he couldn't just sit back and let her leave. Not without trying his utmost to get her back.

He'd made a mistake, yes. He wouldn't make excuses for why. He'd just try to make her see how sorry he was for hurting her, and he'd try hard to never do it again.

If she loved him as she said she did, wouldn't she give him another chance?

But how?

Chapter Twenty-Four: God Has a Plan

Matchmaking Moms of Oceanview Church

THE DAY AFTER WINSTON'S betrayal, Tina dragged herself out of bed, showered away all trace of sadness on her face and convinced herself to go to work. Why not? She had nowhere else to go, and maybe the animals would help her heart heal.

She played music in the car, a strategy to keep her mind off yesterday's events. When she got to the office and wound her way through to the lab space in the back, she'd convinced herself that to the outside world, she looked fine.

That was until Beth glanced up from her work and said, "What's wrong with you?"

Blinking, she said, "Why?"

Beth shrugged. "I don't know, you're not your normal perky self today."

Tina sighed. So much for getting Winston out of her system after twenty-four hours. It was obviously going to take longer than that.

She continued to go into work for the next three days, forcing a pleasant smile on her face. Fake it till you make it, she remembered, a motto she'd often employed in college during the throes of her dating disasters.

On the fourth day, her mood shifted. Up till now, she'd wanted complete distance from Winston. If he'd called, she would've hung up on him. If he'd texted, she would've deleted it.

But he hadn't called. He hadn't texted.

Was he giving up on her that quickly? One argument and he hit the rails? She shook her head as she worked. Then she was right about him after all. Not worth her time. Not worth her love.

She plowed through her lab samples, her mind whirring, her thoughts confusing her. She hadn't actually told him they were breaking up. But in those first few days, she'd known in her heart she had to do it. If she couldn't trust him about something like this, what else was he untrustworthy about? She'd been through this way too many times with guys she liked. She knew what needed to be done.

But now, on Day 4, the thought of a breakup made her sad. Maybe they could work this out? Is that what her heart was telling her? Yet, she was obviously alone in her thoughts because he was a complete No-Show.

She set down the vial she'd been working with and huffed with exasperation. Why were her emotions roller coasting? In the past, when a boy had betrayed her, she'd cut the ties immediately and never looked back. But with Winston, her brain was fighting her heart. Her brain wanted to cut ties. Her heart didn't.

Forgiveness. The word floated to her mind out of nowhere.

She stood from her lab stool, stretched her arms over her head. She pulled out her phone and accessed her online Bible. She searched for forgiveness to see what God had to say on the subject. She paged through till she found the one she was looking for in Corinthians. "If anyone has caused you grief, you ought to forgive and comfort him, so that he will not be overwhelmed with excessive sorrow. I urge you to reaffirm your love for him."

She stared at the words on the tiny screen so long that they swam in front of her. The Bible was incredible, wasn't it? Every concern, every question we had in life could be answered right here.

Was this an answer to the question in her heart about Winston?

She walked to a folding chair in the far corner of the lab and sank into it. Closing her eyes, she prayed to God, not in words, but just letting her thoughts and confusions rise to Him. He knew what she was thinking. She didn't have to ask. She just needed to listen.

She needed His guidance to work through this. And after concentrating for some time, she felt a breakthrough. An illumination.

She had drawn a curtain around her heart to protect herself. She had treated Winston like all her past boyfriends who had hurt her. But he wasn't like them. Winston was not only the first man she'd fallen in love with. He was the first one she'd been with since giving her life over to God.

God had led the two of them together and they already had His protection.

Her eyes popped open, her heart racing. She didn't need to pull herself away from Winston and protect herself from him. She needed to forgive him!

She jumped to her feet. She had to take care of this now. She was certain God had answered her prayer. She headed out to the front desk, searching for Gabrielle to ask for a few hours leave. There she stood. "Gabrielle, I ..."

"There you are. There's a patient in Room 3 asking for you specifically."

Tina sighed, exasperated. She needed to take care of work, then she'd go find Winston to explain. First things first. "Okay, thank you." She absentmindedly took a folder from Gabrielle's hand and headed to Room 3.

She opened the door. In her mind she heard a choir of angels while her eyes absorbed the reality of the person standing in the exam room.

It was Winston.

She closed her eyes and let out a silent chorus of gratitude to God. "Winston ...," she began, and then looked down to the floor. "Rebel!" She knelt and took the dog's bandaged front leg into her hands. "What happened to Rebel?"

He was down on his knees in an instant, beside her, close enough for her to smell the soap and shampoo he'd used this morning. "Nothing."

She was unwrapping the bandage, had gotten to the leg underneath, was carefully fingering it and saw that he was right. "Nothing?"

"Tina, I had to have a reason to get in here to talk to you. So I wrapped a bandage around Rebel and asked to see you here. In this enclosed room. Just the two of us. Well, the three of us," he said, gesturing at his dog who was now covering her entire face with animated licks. "Can you give me two minutes?" He gazed at her expectantly.

"Winston," she started, but he interrupted, his words escaping in a heated rush.

"I didn't tell you about the whole Win4U thing. I'm sorry. I should have. But I didn't know how you would take it. And I figured that because I was quitting the game anyway, it didn't matter. But I was wrong. It did matter. It made you doubt my honesty. It made you think you couldn't trust me. I'm really sorry."

"Winston," she said again.

"When I met you, you pulled me out of a long slump. Because of you, I started seeing how much more life could be, and you reminded me that God had a plan for me. I just needed to leave my old ways behind and look forward. And I will still do that, but it would be so much better if you were by my side."

Tears stung her eyes again, but this time not because she was sad. Because one truth became clear. Just as God had spoken to her about forgiveness, He had spoken to Winston too. They were a couple because God had placed them together. Who was she to break them apart?

"I forgive you," she blurted, and then lifted her hands, cradling his face. "You're a good man, a godly man and I love you. I fell back on old habits that never worked to begin with. That was a mistake. I am so sorry I did that to you. From now on, we work through issues together. And we always let God lead the way."

A beautiful smile covered his face, that handsome face that she'd missed. The face she'd hopefully be looking at for the rest of her life. "From now on?" he asked. "Does that mean we're still together?"

She nodded, her words trapped in her happy smile, and then, in their kiss. He pressed his lips against hers and the warmth that had been missing the last few days was restored.

• • • •

THE END
What happens next, you ask?
Start reading this excerpt from the first chapter of
<u>Finding Love for the Workaholic</u>[1]

• • • •

ISABELLE HARMON DREW in a lungful of air. Holding it for a count of three, she blew it slowly out. In, out, in, out to make her anxiety subside. It was a trick she was familiar with, necessary since childhood. Definitely in college. And grad school. And in her career as a Public Relations Executive? More times than she could count.

In one two three. Out one two three.

Maybe she should throw in a yoga stretch, right here behind her desk. Looking down at her slim snug skirt, she decided against it. Soon the beneficial effects of bringing air into her lungs became apparent. Her chest was less constricted, her pulse slowing and her mind clearer.

As many times as she'd employed the deep breathing ploy during her decade-long career here at Pearson and Thomas, she'd never used it for this particular reason before.

She finished placing a few personal items in her shoulder bag, logged off her company-owned laptop and grabbed the

---

1. https://www.amazon.com/Finding-Workaholic-Matchmaking-Oceanview-Church-ebook/dp/B086NQGL4R/

box of cupcakes. Smoothing her long blonde hair with her palm, she left her office.

A few minutes later she walked into the large conference room located in the center of the second floor of their eight-story office building. Pearson and Thomas PR was the largest Public Relations firm in the Myrtle Beach area and they counted many hotels, vacation resorts and restaurants among their esteemed clients. Isabelle had loved working her way up the food chain, so to speak, delivering profitable PR plans for her clients. She had absolutely loved being at the top, managing the other PR professionals on staff while hobnobbing at industry events and snagging new customers for the firm. But she had never been one to hang around because it was comfortable. Or easy. The challenge was gone, and now, so she would be.

She wondered if anyone would be surprised.

She wondered if anyone would miss her when she was gone.

She found her customary seat in the board room and settled in. She pulled the top off the bakery box and positioned it close by.

Her boss Jose gave her an eyebrow up silent greeting when he entered the room. Jose had never been particularly warm and fuzzy to her, but after her surprise announcement in his office earlier this morning, he had no reason to make her feel comfortable. She'd asked for five minutes at the end of this meeting and he'd begrudgingly agreed. She knew he'd rather have sent a cold email to staff, but she wanted to handle this her way.

An hour later, the staff meeting of the firm's executives had gone off without a hitch. When her six fellow execs were gathering up their papers, closing their laptops and getting to their feet, Isabelle raised a finger. "One more thing before you leave, everyone. Five minutes please?"

Considering the only thing standing between them and lunch was Isabelle's five-minute delay, a few of them rolled their eyes while a few more groaned. Good-naturedly, she hoped.

"It won't take any longer than five minutes, I promise. And you'll get a cupcake out of the deal." She gestured to the box that had been sitting beside her for the last hour.

A few appreciative noises now. Okay, she had their attention.

"In this box, I have sixteen cupcakes. Nine with chocolate frosting and seven with vanilla frosting." She lifted the box and tilted it so they could all see. "As you notice, each cupcake has a single letter written on it. Your job is to break into two teams and focus on arranging the cupcake letters into an announcement that makes sense."

They were intrigued, she could tell by the fact that they didn't complain. "Quickly, break into teams and I'll give you your next step."

They were professionals and they'd been through their share of team building exercises, so they quickly split into two teams of three gathered on opposite sides of the conference table. Jose didn't join in. Of course, Isabelle didn't expect him to.

"Good. This team, you have the chocolate cupcakes." She pulled out all nine and set them on the table in front of them. She walked to the far side of the table. "This team, you have the vanilla cupcakes." She did the same with their seven cupcakes. She pulled out her phone and glanced at the time. "We've used

FINDING LOVE FOR THE LONER   219

roughly one minute for set-up which means you have four minutes to work together and solve your puzzle. I'll set the stopwatch. Ready? Go."

She watched them with an affectionate tilt to her lips. She loved this team, she really did. They'd done great things together. Her ambivalence toward Jose notwithstanding, it wasn't necessarily his leadership that was driving her out. Not really. Although she was quite sure she could've done a better job as the one in charge, she had to look at his selection realistically and concede that at the time he was hired, three years ago, she probably wasn't seasoned enough to take over the head slot. They'd brought him in from outside the company with, reportedly, loads of experience. The fact that she never saw clear evidence of that, made her more than a little dejected.

No, Jose notwithstanding, it was simply time to move on. That's all. No hard feelings, no big blow up. Just taking her talents and ambitions somewhere else.

Quiet engaged teamwork was evolving into surprised noises as the puzzles were being solved. She checked her stopwatch. "How are we doing? Did you solve the puzzle? Did you?"

Her answer came in outbursts of "What?" "You're kidding!" "You're leaving?"

Isabelle smiled and walked to the chocolate team. "Please read the cupcakes. Sam?"

"I'm leaving." His monotone told her exactly what her buddy Sam thought about this news. "But there's no apostrophe."

She chuckled and strode to the other side of the room. "Vanilla team?"

"Good-bye." A coworker named Tom turned to her and raised a pointed eyebrow. "No hyphen."

She smiled and pointed at him. "The hyphen is optional." She moved to the middle of the table and raised her hands to them. "It's true. I want to tell you how much I've enjoyed working with all of you, creating campaigns to help our clients get their word out and raise their bottom line. It's been a dream job and you have been a dream team. But now it's time for me to move on. So, thank you for all your friendship."

At least four of the exec team started talking at the same time, words garbled, rising to the ceiling. Then she heard someone say, "Why?"

She let the word reverberate in the conference room and then shrugged. "I'm going to do something different. I have an idea in mind for my own business and after much thought I decided to give it a try. I'll either fail or I'll succeed but I'll never know if I don't leave behind all that's familiar and just ... go for it."

"What is it?"

"What will you be doing?"

She let the questions hang there for a minute, deciding just how honest to be with them. Finally, she decided total honesty was best, because her coworkers and friends in this room wished the best for her and deserved it. "I don't have it fully fleshed out yet. But I know I have a passion for food. And entertainment. And the camaraderie that people form while sitting around a big table, eating a great meal and drinking good wine and getting to know each other. And I want to help people feel that magic."

One of the men in the room frowned, his bottom lip out. "So ... you're opening a restaurant?" and his dubious tone fin-

FINDING LOVE FOR THE LONER

ished his unspoken thought ... there's a million of them out there already.

"Nope. Not a restaurant."

"Then what?"

"Something creative. Something new. I'm going to inject myself into new age ways to get the word out to people. I'm going to become an influencer in the culinary-slash-entertainment community. I'll start here in Myrtle Beach and eventually go broader. My business plan is not fully set yet. But that's part of why I'm excited. So that I can follow the path as it presents itself. The opportunities are endless."

Marjorie, the one she'd worked with the longest and had formed the closest friendship with said, "Oh wow. I have a million ideas running through my head. A blog filled with beautiful pictures of food. Original recipes. Social media. Videos."

Isabelle smiled, nodding her head as Marjorie threw out ideas. "Yes. And more. A million more. I'm not going to say no to anything that makes sense to grow my business."

Marjorie gave her a smile. "All you need is for some of your stuff to go viral and you're all set. Maybe a cooking show on the Food Network?"

Isabelle gave an exaggerated shrug. "I'm open to it all."

The five minutes had slipped by and the people were starting to head out. "Take the cupcakes! A couple each!"

She stepped over to the door so she could offer a quick handshake or hug to each of them, along with a personal goodbye. Marjorie lingered and gave her a long hug. She pulled away and Isabelle could see a tear in her eye. "Now, don't...."

Marjorie sniffed. "Okay. I'm just going to miss you, you know?"

"Just because I won't be in the office doesn't mean we can't see each other."

"Yeah, that's true," she said dubiously. "Will you stay in touch? What if I set up a monthly lunch? Would you come?"

"Of course! I promise." She patted her friend on the shoulder.

"If anyone can make their entrepreneurial dream come true, it would be you."

The vote of confidence made a tear sting at Isabelle's eye. She couldn't have that, crying during her final few minutes of her PR career.

• • • •

Don't Miss Out! Get all the Matchmaking Moms' adventures:

Matchmaking Moms of Oceanview Church series:

BOOK 1: *Meet the Moms*[1]: A prologue novella to kick off the series. Dahlia, Lily and Rose form a team of covert matchmakers to find love where their adult children have failed. Will the moms find love for Winston the Loner, Isabelle the Workaholic and Micah the Playboy and remain in the shadows?

BOOK 2: *Finding Love for the Loner*[2]: Lily's son Winston has made a solitary life centered around his job, his dog Rebel and

---

1. https://www.amazon.com/Meet-Moms-Matchmaking-Oceanview-Church-ebook/dp/B086N3Z58H/

2. https://www.amazon.com/Finding-Loner-Matchmaking-Oceanview-Church-ebook/dp/B086N51QRL/

his online videogaming prowess. Will Rose the matchmaker find his love in fellow dog-lover Tina, and will Tina be able to steal his heart?

BOOK 3: *Finding Love for the Workaholic*:[3] A successful match is under their belts! An independent and successful businesswoman, Rose's daughter Isabelle knows the type of man she's looking for. Can matchmaker Dahlia make her realize that photographer Zach may not be what she's looking for, but may just be her perfect match?

BOOK 4: *Finding Love for the Playboy*:[4] The Matchmaking Moms face their toughest challenge yet. Dahlia's son, talent

---

3. https://www.amazon.com/Finding-Workaholic-Matchmaking-Oceanview-Church-ebook/dp/B086NQGL4R/

FINDING LOVE FOR THE LONER

agent Micah rubs elbows with Hollywood's elite, always with a beautiful woman on his arm. But matchmaker Lily knows the secret to finding his one-and-only match and it's single mom, Maria.

BOOK 5: *Finding Love for the Matchmaker*:[5] The Matchmaking Moms throw a party to reveal their secret efforts. But is it possible that they weren't quite as covert as they thought? Did the matches turn the tables and actually find love for one of the matchmakers?

---

4. https://www.amazon.com/Finding-Playboy-Matchmaking-Oceanview-Church-ebook/dp/B086NP81WR/

5. https://www.amazon.com/Finding-Matchmaker-Matchmaking-Oceanview-Church-ebook/dp/B086NQW85F/

Leave a Review!

Did you enjoy *Finding Love for the Loner*? Please help guide other Christian fiction readers to find it and enjoy it too. Click right here[1] and leave a review!

---

1. https://www.amazon.com/Finding-Loner-Matchmaking-Oceanview-Church-ebook/dp/B086N51QRL/

Find Laurie online

Subscribe to Laurie's monthly newsletter[1] for exclusive news, giveaways and contests.
Visit Laurie's website[2] for a broader look at all her work.
Follow her on Facebook.[3]
Follow her on Bookbub.[4]
Follow her on Amazon[5].

What has Laurie written besides Matchmaking Moms?

---

1. https://www.authorlaurielarsen.com/reader-group
2. https://www.authorlaurielarsen.com/
3. https://www.facebook.com/authorlaurielarsen
4. https://www.bookbub.com/profile/laurie-larsen
5. https://www.amazon.com/Laurie-Larsen/e/B007GR-LY0A?ref=sr_ntt_srch_lnk_1&qid=1586186414&sr=8-1

The Murrells Inlet Miracles series:

BOOK 1: Sanctuary[1]: Successful Philadelphia attorney Nora Ramsey never even knew there was another life for her before Aunt Edie left her with her ramshackle mansion and once-thriving horse business. Veterinarian Shaw Flynn seems a partner, then a love interest, before finding out his deepest and darkest secret.

BOOK 2: Restoration[2]: Young, single mom Carly Milner was making it on her own raising her toddler Grace and finishing

---

1. https://books2read.com/u/bOrgro

2. https://books2read.com/u/m2o5k6

her education so she could launch her professional career. When the love of her life, Ryan Melrose returns, wanting a place in Grace's life, can she ever trust him again?

BOOK 3: Crescendo[3]: Multi-award winner! A rags to riches story in the world of country music, with a twist! Black sheep in a wealthy family Haley Witherspoon has finally found the career that brings her passion, and it's with handsome aspiring country musician, Blake Scott. Can they overcome her family's disapproval, his own internal guilt, mounting danger from a fan to achieve success?

• • • •

---

3. https://books2read.com/u/brGegZ

BOOK 4: Capsized[4]: God "overseas" everything. Two highly competitive extreme athletes pair up to achieve victory in the world of competitive yacht sailing. With physical attraction tempting them, Sadie and Jett must keep their eyes on the prize. But God has other plans. As they face adversity and danger, will God's will have them racing toward one another instead of the glory of the win?

BOOK 5: Seized:[5] Gloria's gig raising her two orphaned nephews is done. With God's help, Blake and Brent are flour-

---

4. https://books2read.com/u/b62AQE

5. https://books2read.com/u/4AQZo0

FINDING LOVE FOR THE LONER

ishing in their own lives and she now faces an empty nest. Spreading her wings and finding a love of her own sounds pretty good until Alejandro, the cop she falls in love with, inadvertently leads an escaped convict to her door, one with a vendetta against him.

MURRELLS INLET MIRACLES boxset[6]: first three books in one easy download!

---

6. https://books2read.com/u/mVQDd5

The Pawleys Island Paradise series:

BOOK 1: <u>Roadtrip to Redemption</u>[1]. *It started as a trip to lose old memories. It became a journey to find her heart.* A woman facing the most desolate summer of her life, follows God's direction and instead has the most rewarding and life-changing summer of all.

BOOK 2: Tide to Atonement[2]. *Life knocked him down. Faith raised him up.* A man has paid his debt to society and is released from prison. Determined to create a life to be proud of, he re-

---

1. https://books2read.com/u/3L9Vee

2. https://books2read.com/u/4EDNAM

alizes his past isn't quite as willing to be done as he wants it to be.

BOOK 3: Journey to Fulfillment[3]. *A traumatic family event. Distinctly opposite ways of dealing with it between husband and wife. Let no man put asunder.* A married couple deals with a family tragedy in different ways and works through the resulting collapse of their marriage to reconcile their love for each other.

BOOK 4: Bridge to Fruition[4]. *The old is gone. The new is come.* A young woman from an affluent family finds love with a man

---

3. https://books2read.com/u/bwWyzv

4. https://books2read.com/u/4Xo0BL

who grew up in the foster system. Can they let go of the trappings of their past and find love together in their present?

BOOK 5: Path to Discovery[5]. A brokenhearted New York actress welcomes the escape from the hustle and bustle of the big city to take the lead in a beach-town dinner theater show. It's the solace and sanctuary that she's needed ever since her world came crumbling down. But then he walks in... back into her life and her memories of her worst nightmare.

BOOK 6: Return to Devotion[6]. *Can men and women be "just friends?"* A military wife deals with unbearable loneliness on

---

5. https://books2read.com/u/4NRorx

6. https://books2read.com/u/49PVpk

FINDING LOVE FOR THE LONER

her husband's third overseas deployment, leading to an indiscretion with her new male friend. Will the truth destroy everything she and her husband have built as man and wife?

BOOK 7: Pawleys Island Paradise: A Companion[7]. Discover the stories and inspiration that led to the Pawleys Island Paradise series! A short, fully-illustrated non-fiction companion to the beloved Pawleys Island Paradise series of inspirational romance by award-winning author Laurie Larsen.

PAWLEYS Island Paradise boxset[8]: First three books in one easy download!

---

7. https://www.authorlaurielarsen.com/a-companion-nonfiction

8. https://books2read.com/u/3L9N9w

PREACHER MAN[9]. Laurie's 2010 EPIC Award winner for Best Spiritual Romance of 2010: A beautiful, heartwarming Christian love story that will leave you feeling good.

Made in the USA
Columbia, SC
08 July 2020